"You really do believe my brother was murdered?" Heather asked.

Tyler nodded. "I do. Whatever information he had found about the drug mastermind cost him his life."

And now put her and her son in danger.

She shook her head. "No, *you* cost him his life. You pushed him to do something he wasn't trained to do."

The sharp tip of her barb hit him squarely in the gut. "A fact I will have to live with," Tyler stated with more regret than she could possibly know. "Believe me, I wish I had done things differently."

Tyler had been doing his job. A job that wasn't finished. "If I am going to bring his murderers to justice, I need to find the notebook he told me he had."

She held his gaze. "That's why you broke into the house."

"I didn't break in. As I said, your brother gave me a key. He'd said if anything happened to him that I'd find what I needed here at the farm."

Well, something had happened. Something terrible. And he wasn't going to let *anything* happen to Heather and her boy.

Terri Reed's romance and romantic suspense novels have appeared on *Publishers Weekly* top twenty-five and Nielsen BookScan's top one hundred lists and have been featured in *USA TODAY*, *Christian Fiction Magazine* and *RT Book Reviews*. Her books have finaled in the Romance Writers of America RITA® Award contest, the National Readers' Choice Award contest and three times in the American Christian Fiction Writers' Carol Award contest. Contact Terri at terrireed.com or PO Box 19555, Portland, OR 97224.

Books by Terri Reed

Love Inspired Suspense

Northern Border Patrol

Danger at the Border
Joint Investigation
Murder Under the Mistletoe

Capitol K-9 Unit

Duty Bound Guardian

Protection Specialists

The Innocent Witness
The Secret Heiress
The Doctor's Defender
The Cowboy Target

The McClains

Double Deception
Double Jeopardy
Double Cross
Double Threat Christmas

Visit the Author Profile page at Harlequin.com for more titles.

MURDER UNDER THE MISTLETOE

TERRI REED

HARLEQUIN® LOVE INSPIRED® SUSPENSE

Recycling programs
for this product may
not exist in your area.

™ LOVE INSPIRED BOOKS

ISBN-13: 978-0-373-44703-9

Murder Under the Mistletoe

Copyright © 2015 by Terri Reed

www.Harlequin.com

Printed in U.S.A.

Every good and perfect gift is from above,
coming down from the Father of the heavenly lights,
who does not change like shifting shadows.
—*James* 1:17

This book is dedicated to my family for all the support and love you give me every day. God blessed me greatly with a wonderful husband and two fabulous kids.

ONE

"Good night, sweet boy." Heather Larson-Randall leaned in to kiss her six-year-old son's forehead.

"Night, Mommy." Colin snuggled deeper beneath the thick comforter. He lay in the twin-size bed in the room that once had been Heather's.

Gone were the decorations of her adolescence—posters of the latest celebrity heartthrob and her 4-H ribbons and trophies. It had taken the past three days to transform the room in a superhero motif that would have made Ken, her late husband, proud.

A cold draft skated across the back of her neck. The late November night had grown chilly, but at least the northern Idaho rain had abated for now. The weatherman had predicted a drop in temperature over the next few days. Fitting for this year's Thanksgiving. She just needed to get through the day for Colin's sake. Then she could concentrate on Christmas.

Hopefully celebrating the birth of Jesus would take her mind off her brother's tragic death.

She also hoped they had snow by Christmas morning. Colin loved the snow. And, as always, her life's priority was Colin.

She moved to the bedroom door. The creak of the

old farmhouse's hardwood floor beneath her feet followed each of her steps, echoing the hollow, lonely beat
of her heart.

"Mommy?"

Pausing in the doorway with her hand hovering over
the light switch, she smiled patiently at her son. Colin
looked so much like Ken with his dark brown hair falling over one eye and his dimpled chin. She ached with
love for her son and regret that he'd never know his father. "Yes, sweetie?"

Her late parents had taught her that replacing the
word *what* with the more positive *yes* when talking to
children created a strong, effective bond. The proof was
in how close her family had been.

Colin's big blue-green eyes stared at her intently.
"Do you think Uncle Seth is with Daddy and Grandma
and Grandpa?"

The innocent question speared through her like a hot
poker. She bit the inside of her cheek to keep the tears
of grief at bay. Five years ago, just before Colin's first
birthday, her husband had been killed while serving
his country in Afghanistan, leaving Heather to raise
their son alone. She'd made sure every day that Colin
knew his father had loved him. Adding to her grief, her
parents had been killed in a freak car accident when
Colin was four.

Now, two years later and five days ago, she'd lost
her younger brother, Seth, to what appeared to be a
cocaine overdose.

She struggled to comprehend how Seth had fallen
back into using drugs after being clean the past couple
of years. He'd had so much going for him. A fiancée he
adored, half the tree farm and a bright future. She didn't
know what had sent him running back to the abyss.

Placing one hand on her chest, she leaned against the doorjamb, needing the strength of her childhood home to keep her upright when the grief pressing down on her threatened to send her to the floor in a heap. "Yes, dear. I'm sure they are all together."

A familiar tide of anger washed over her. Anger at God for allowing the tragedies that had left her and Colin alone in the world. On the heels of the anger came a flood of guilt for blaming God. Sometimes it was hard to cling to her faith when the world tried to knock her down.

The cell phone in the pocket of her plush robe buzzed.

"I'll come back to check on you in a bit," she told Colin, then flipped off the light and stepped into the dimly lit hallway to answer the phone.

"Hello?"

"Your brother's death isn't what it seems," a rough, low voice said into her ear, sending a chill down her spine. "Leave the farm. It's not safe."

Her breath hitched; her mind reeled. "What? Who is this?"

The line beeped, then went silent.

A tremor from deep inside worked its way out of her. *Leave the farm. It's not safe.*

She put a hand on the wall to steady herself, feeling the familiar fuzzy velvet texture of the flock wallpaper. This couldn't be happening, not now with Seth's death hanging over her like a cloud of doom.

His death had been ruled an accidental overdose.

Even if she wanted to leave the farm, she and Colin had nowhere to go. The day she had learned of Seth's death, she'd given up her job and the apartment in Washington State to move back to Idaho.

Now the Christmas tree farm was her and Colin's only home. Their livelihood. Without the farm she wasn't sure what would happen to them.

Seeds of fear burrowed in her chest and took root. She quickly made her way downstairs, checking that the doors were securely locked. She peered out the front picture window. The full moon, big and round and shining brightly, bathed the sea of Douglas fir, grand fir and noble fir trees stretching over forty acres of land on the tree farm that had been in her family for three generations.

Long shadows obscured the front drive. The other work buildings on the farm were dark, as well. The small cabins that provided lodging for the seasonal employees couldn't be seen through the thick grove of trees, creating a sense of isolation that had never bothered her when she was growing up here.

But she'd never had a menacing phone call before now.

Suddenly movement on the fringe between the trees and the wide expanse of lawn caught her eye. Then the shadow shifted and disappeared. Had she really seen something out there? Or was fear making her paranoid?

She yanked the curtains closed. Surely she was imagining things. Satisfied the house was locked up tight, she hurried back upstairs to the master bedroom that had once belonged to her parents and her grandparents before them. Though she'd replaced her parents' belongings with her own, she still considered the room theirs.

Sitting on the edge of the bed, she called the local sheriff's office and told the answering sergeant about the disturbing call. She couldn't be sure she'd seen anything in the shadows of the trees, so she kept that to herself. Because there was no immediate threat, the sergeant promised to send a deputy over in the morning.

Not at all reassured, she hung up and crawled into bed. She held her phone to her chest. Right now she wished she'd given in to Colin's pleas for a dog. Tomorrow she would go to the local animal shelter and find a nice big canine with a loud bark.

She leaned back against the pillows, her gaze landing on the picture of her parents hanging on the opposite wall. Her mother had been so beautiful and her father so handsome. But more important, they'd been great parents to her and Seth, providing a stable home and love. Lots of love.

The very things she wanted to give Colin.

Somehow none of that had been enough to keep Seth from turning to drugs. She didn't know what had driven him to seek the high of narcotics when he was younger. Or more recently. The not knowing ate at her. He'd refused to talk about the dark days of his addiction. Heather had hoped one day he'd realize she loved him no matter what.

Maybe if she'd stayed closer to home rather than leaving for college, Seth wouldn't have turned into a junkie. Maybe if she'd begged, Ken would have left the army. Maybe if she'd been with her parents that night, they wouldn't have died in that accident. Maybe, maybe, maybe.

She turned off the light and lay in the dark. She wanted to pray for God to protect them and lessen the burden of guilt she carried. But her prayers for Ken's safety had gone unanswered. Why would God listen to her now?

Her eyelids grew heavy. Her head bobbed as sleep's greedy hands pulled her into slumber.

A soft thud jolted her fully awake. Her heart nearly exploded with fright. She bolted from the bed and strained to listen.

Nothing.

Maybe it had been Colin getting up to use the bathroom. Yes, that had to be it. She sucked in air and slowly released her breath, working to calm her frantic pulse. She glanced at the clock. She'd slept for three hours.

After pulling on her robe, she padded quietly down the hall to check on her son. The bathroom was dark and empty. She moved on to his room. The moon's glow streamed through the open curtains, revealing Colin fast asleep. She closed the door and waited. The house was silent now, yet the hairs on her nape rose and chills prickled her skin.

Cautiously, she moved to the top of the stairs and stared into darkness.

Was someone in the house?

Another noise jolted through her, making her tremble. She needed to call for help. As quietly as she could, she raced back to her bedroom and swiped the phone off the bed, then hurried into the hall and stood guard in front of Colin's door. She dialed and when the sergeant answered, she whispered, "This is Heather Randall again. There's someone in my house!"

"Are you sure?" the man asked. "Have you seen an intruder?"

"No, I heard a noise."

He sighed. "Sit tight. I'll send one of the deputies out."

Sit tight? It would take at least thirty minutes for a deputy to reach the farm from Bonners Ferry, the nearest town. Was she supposed to wait and see if the intruder decided to come upstairs? Then what? She had no weapon, no way to defend herself or Colin. She thanked the deputy anyway and hung up.

She couldn't sit there like some insipid victim. She crept slowly down the staircase, careful to avoid the spots that would creak. She knew every inch of this house, knew every board that would betray her presence, every piece of furniture to navigate around in the inky blackness. She made her way to the kitchen.

She glanced at the knife block with the razor-sharp knife set. As tempting as it was to grab a knife to use as a weapon, she knew that wasn't a good choice. A knife could be too easily taken away and used against her. Instead, she moved to the stove.

Careful not to jostle the pans hanging over the range, she grabbed the largest cast-iron skillet. Her mother's favorite. Hefting the heavy pan in her hands like a baseball bat, she crept back to the stairs.

At the bottom step, she waited, listening.

All was quiet. She was being paranoid. The noises she'd heard had been the house settling for the night. All the doors and windows were locked up tight. The phone call had been a mean hoax, meant to frighten her.

Well, it had worked. Her hands tightened around the cold handle of the skillet. She placed one foot on the first step.

A soft knock at the back door echoed in the stillness of the house.

Abandoning the stairs, she pressed her back to the wall. Adjusting her grip more firmly on the skillet's sturdy handle, she inched toward the kitchen. She peered around the corner. The outline of a man shone through the curtained window on the back door.

She *had* seen someone creeping around outside. And now they wanted inside.

Who would come to the farmhouse in the middle of the night? Caution had her refrain from turning on the lights. If she didn't answer the door, would the person go away?

She hoped so.

The person knocked again, louder this time.

Maybe it was the sheriff's deputy. Right, one just happened to be close enough?

It was possible, she supposed. Wary, she approached the door and flipped on the outside porch light. But nothing happened. Great timing to have a burned-out lightbulb at the exact moment she needed the glow.

As indecision on what to do warred within her, the man outside turned the doorknob. She jumped back, prepared to use the skillet to defend herself.

She should retreat and wait upstairs as the sergeant had said. That would be the smart thing to do. But what if the intruder decided to break in? What if he got to her son before the police could arrive?

A surge of protectiveness coursed through her veins. Adrenaline shoved back the fear. She was alone. It was up to her to defend her house, her son. She stood her ground.

The unmistakable sound of a key sliding into the lock and the lock's tumblers turning ratcheted her tension.

She moved swiftly to press her back against the wall next to the door seconds before the door opened and the intruder stepped inside. A small beam of light glowed in the darkness as the man moved forward. Holding her breath, she knew she had the element of surprise on her side and one shot at felling the trespasser. She had to make it count.

Stepping carefully behind the figure, she raised the iron fry pan and swung.

The swoosh of moving air alerted DEA agent Tyler Griffin to an impending attack. He spun around, the penlight dropping to the ground, and raised an arm to deflect the blow. He was too late. Something hard and solid glanced off his elbow and connected with his head, sending pain shooting in all directions through his body.

The crack to his noggin sent him staggering backward until his back hit the dining room table. He toppled sideways into a sprawling heap on the floor. His elbow throbbed all the way to his shoulder.

He shook his head, trying to regain his equilibrium. He could barely make out the dark form of a body standing a few feet away. He wrenched his sidearm from the holster attached to his belt. "Halt! DEA!"

His shout didn't quite have the normal amount of punch it usually held.

The figure retreated a few steps.

Tyler blinked back the spots and aimed. His finger hovered near the trigger, but he couldn't keep his assailant in focus long enough to fire.

The sudden glare of the overhead light blinded him. With a sinking feeling, he realized he made an easy target if his assailant decided to finish him off. This wasn't the way he'd pictured his life ending.

But, then again, he wasn't in control of life's happenings. He'd learned that long ago. The best he could do was pray that if God wanted to take him now, that it was quick and painless.

"You're a cop?"

The distinctly female voice had him blinking rapidly to adjust to the light. He lowered his sidearm. His gaze fixed on the woman standing by the back door he'd just come through. She held a large black cast-iron skillet in her hands, looking as if she were ready to take another swing at his head.

He nearly laughed out loud. He'd allowed an assailant to get the drop on him. A woman with a frying pan, at that. Man, he must be suffering burnout.

He could only imagine the ribbing he'd suffer when his fellow agents found out he'd been clocked by a raven-haired beauty in a fuzzy yellow robe and... Were those toe socks?

Her tangle of thick ebony curls cascaded about her shoulders like a cloud, and the most amazing hazel eyes regarded him with stark fear. Her gaze moved to the gun in his hand, then back to meet his scrutiny.

Forcing himself to a sitting position, he reholstered his weapon and let his head sink into his hands with a groan. "You hit me."

"I'll do it again if you don't tell me who you are and what you're doing here and how you have a key to my house," she growled.

Feisty, considering he'd had her at gunpoint. Lifting his head, he started at the sight of his hands covered with blood. Apparently the knock over the head with the pan had broken the skin on his scalp. Hopefully, that was the only thing she'd broken.

He reached for his ID wallet and held it up for her to see. "Agent Tyler Griffin, DEA. You must be Heather."

One lip curled up. "Obviously." Her dark winged brows dipped as she took a step closer to inspect his credentials. She danced back and frowned. "How do I know that's real, and how do you know my name?"

"It's real. You can check it out if you'd like." He held the leather case out for her to take. "There's a number on the card you can call."

"Throw it over."

Smart, too. He liked that. He tossed it so it landed at her feet. Keeping her focus on him, she picked the wallet up. Her straight white teeth tugged on her bottom lip. "You didn't answer me. How did you get a key, and how do you know who I am?"

"Your brother."

Her eyes narrowed. "What?"

"Seth gave me the key." Tyler probed the tender spot on his head. "He was working with us."

Disbelief skipped across her lovely face. "Right. Seth was working with the DEA? Why would he give you a key to the house?"

"Yes, he was working for us." He cringed. He loathed explaining why he had the key, but there was no help for it. He had to tell her. "He gave me the key in case anything happened to him."

"I don't believe you. The sheriff's on his way."

Perfect. Could this operation get any more complicated? They'd purposely kept the local law out of the loop in case there was corruption within the department. Tyler hadn't wanted to blow his confidential informant's identity.

He mentally snorted as the sharp blade of guilt twisted in his gut. Seth's cover had been blown just the same.

"Look, call the number on the card. Then we'll talk."

"Put your gun on the floor and kick it over to me," she said, her eyes sparking with challenge and distrust.

"No way. That's not how this works." An agent never handed over his firearm. He stood. The world swam. His vision blurred. He reached out for the desk and missed.

He toppled face-first onto the floor and fell into darkness.

Oh, no. He'd passed out. Or had she killed him?

Horrified by either prospect, Heather remained rooted to the floor. Her first impulse was to help him. But the need to protect her son was a fierce force, urging her to turn tail and run, grab Colin and head for the car.

She couldn't leave the intruder lying there without making sure he wasn't dead. Or that he didn't die from the wound she'd given him. She would not feel guilty for clobbering him with the pan.

Stuffing his wallet into the deep pocket of her robe, she tentatively moved closer. Her foot bumped up against the gun holstered at his hip. Carefully, she slipped the weapon from the leather holster and clicked on the safety before tucking it into her pocket next to his ID.

Her muscles and nerves tensed, on high alert, ready to jump away if he so much as twitched. He didn't move. She laid two fingers against his neck. His pulse beat with a strong rhythm. *Good.* He wasn't dead, only unconscious.

Which wasn't good. She'd probably given him a concussion.

She gently turned him onto his back. He'd made an intimidating picture awake, but now with his features relaxed, she noticed the chiseled strength of his jaw, the angles and planes of his brow and cheekbones. *Handsome.* Though his eyelids were closed now, she'd noticed his striking blue eyes were the color of the sky on a clear day.

He had to be at least six feet tall. The black cargo pants and black long-sleeved T-shirt beneath the leather jacket showed off a well-conditioned physique. Was he really a drug enforcement agent? What did he mean, Seth had been working for them?

She grabbed a kitchen towel and used the material as a makeshift bandage for the laceration on his scalp. Then, after undoing the ties to the dining room chair cushion, she slid the cushion off the seat, gently lifted the injured, unconscious man's head and slipped the pillow beneath him. His eyelids popped open. Startled, she scuttled back and slipped a hand into her pocket to cradle the gun there.

Keeping a close watch on him, she called the number on the card placed opposite his badge inside the brown leather case and even though the man that answered identified himself as Deputy Director Moore, she asked, "How do I know you're who you say you are?"

The agent sat up and rubbed his head. She stared him down, and he met her gaze, waiting.

"Excuse me? Who is this?" Irritation threaded through the tone of the man on the other end of the line.

Not willing to give her name, she said, "I've a man here claiming he's a DEA agent and that you are his boss. But how do I know you two aren't in league together and this isn't some elaborate scam?"

"Madame, call this number." The man rattled off a ten-digit number. Thankful for the memorization skills she'd learned in college, she put the number to memory. "You can confirm for yourself who I am. Once you have, ring me back." The man hung up.

Still disbelieving, she input the number into the phone and waited a moment until a woman answered, "Department of Homeland Security, how may I direct your call?"

Surprised, she hesitated, then hung up. Was this for real? Homeland Security? No way.

She quickly called 411 and asked for the main number of the Department of Homeland Security. The automated voice gave her the same number that she'd just dialed.

Stunned but not quite ready to accept that the man sitting on the floor watching her was really law enforcement, she redialed the number for Homeland Security and asked to speak to Deputy Director Moore.

"The deputy director is not in at the moment. Would you care to leave a name and number for when he returns?"

Heather chewed on her bottom lip for a second before she said, "Uh, can you tell me if there is an agent name Tyler Griffin working for the DEA?"

"I'm not at liberty to give out that information. Did you want to leave a message for the deputy director?"

"No, that's okay." Heather hung up.

Tyler arched an eyebrow at her.

She narrowed her gaze and redialed Deputy Director Moore's direct line. He answered on the first ring.

The man confirmed his agent's identity. The relief was unexpected. At least she didn't have to fear the agent was there to hurt her.

"Let me speak to Agent Griffin," the gruff man on the phone demanded.

She squatted down next to Tyler and handed him the phone. "He wants to talk to you."

Tyler held the phone to his ear. "Griffin here."

He listened, his mouth pressing into a grim line. "Yes, sir. I understand, sir. The local sheriff is on his way here. Thank you, sir." He pressed the end button. "My boss will be in contact with the sheriff's department." He held out the phone. "Are you satisfied?"

"I suppose." Her fingers curled around the phone.

His hand clasped around her wrist.

She let out a little yelp and tried to break his hold. His grip was warm, tight, but not painful.

"Not so fast," he said. His intent gaze held her captive as surely as his hand. "I want my gun back."

Her heart beat wildly. "It's in my pocket." Why did she sound as if she'd run a marathon?

With his free hand, he reached into the pocket of

her robe, retrieved his weapon and jammed it into his holster.

"Uh, you can let go of me now." She stared at the point where his big hand circled her slender wrist. She had no doubt he could break her bones with a quick snap if he chose to.

He let go, holding his hands up, palms out. "Sorry."

"Tell me what you meant when you said my brother was working with you. And why did he think something would happen to him?"

Tyler scrubbed a hand over his jaw. "Your brother informed my office that your family's tree farm was being used to smuggle cocaine into Canada."

She dropped from a squat to her knees. "Cocaine?"

The official ruling in her brother's death flashed in her mind. Overdose of injectable cocaine. She'd had so much trouble accepting the coroner's findings. Seth had been belonephobic. He abhorred sharp objects, especially needles. He'd snorted, smoked and swallowed his drugs.

Plus he'd promised her he was clean. She'd believed him.

However, the sheriff hadn't believed her when she'd claimed Seth wouldn't have injected himself with drugs. She could tell the sheriff had thought she was fooling herself. He'd said junkies would do whatever they could for the high, even overcome a lifelong fear.

Without any evidence to the contrary, she'd had to come to terms with Seth's death as an accident. But now…?

"Someone here on the farm was involved in drug smuggling?" It didn't make sense. "That can't be. Most of our employees have been with us for years. I trust them. I can't imagine any of them partaking in drugs, let alone using our farm for nefarious purposes."

"Not all of your employees are long-term, right? You do have some transient workers."

She chewed on the inside of her lip. An anxious flutter started low in her tummy. "True. We do have a few seasonal laborers who come in the fall and stay until Christmas day. Then they travel back to their homes. But those few have been coming for years, as well."

"You can't always predict what people will do if given the right motivation." He slowly stood.

His words sent a shiver of apprehension crawling across the nape of her neck. She rose to face him. "Where is the cocaine coming from?"

"We don't know the direct route, but we do know the source of the cocaine coming into the US is from Central America. There are many drug cartels in various countries south of the border infiltrating both the US and Canada. And more recently, Australia."

Her mouth went dry. "There's a drug cartel here?"

"Possibly." Tyler sank down on the dining room chair. "I'm working with IBETs—Integrated Border Enforcement Teams—we've been investigating rumors of drugs crossing the US–Canadian border for months. Two weeks ago Seth reached out to me and my team."

Pride filled Heather. She could only imagine how scary it had been for Seth to seek help. Going up against a drug cartel was no small feat.

"Apparently last year he'd needed some extra cash," Tyler continued. "He had allowed a shipment of cocaine to hitch a ride into Canada with a shipment of trees from your farm. He'd thought it was a onetime deal. But when they came back to him this year, he realized he'd gotten in over his head."

Heather silently groaned. One step forward, two steps back. Seth had always courted trouble with his decision making.

"We—" Tyler grimaced "—I convinced him to find out as much as he could and keep a record of everything he learned, including who, what, where and when."

Stunned, Heather rocked back on her heels. "Let me get this straight. My brother came to you with information about an illegal drug operation on our farm and you—" A cold sweat broke out on her skin. "He was spying for you?"

A grim expression stole over Tyler's face. "Yes."

Heather backed away. Her mind scrambled to make sense of what she was hearing. It was one thing for Seth to be a whistle-blower and another entirely for him to play the role of spy. "That was a dangerous thing for you to ask of him."

"Yes, it was."

She stilled as a thought burned through her brain. Her blood turned to ice. "He didn't die of an accidental overdose. Someone killed him."

"That's what I believe."

"He's dead because of you!"

Tyler closed his eyes. When he opened them, the bleakness in his gaze confirmed her accusation. "Yes."

TWO

Tyler held Heather's gaze with what he hoped was dispassion and not the swirling maelstrom of guilt laying siege to his psyche. He wouldn't shirk the responsibility of Seth Larson's murder.

Despite Seth's past addictions, Tyler had sensed his sincere need to get out from under the thumb of the drug cartel. Though Tyler may not have injected Seth with the lethal dose of cocaine, he felt responsible. Tyler had no doubt that someone had found out that Seth was keeping an account of the illegal activities going on at the Larson family Christmas tree farm. And that someone then killed Seth. He gritted his teeth against the throbbing in his head.

Heather stared at him with wide eyes full of flashing anger. "How could you let this happen?"

It was a valid question. One he'd been asking himself for the past five days. One his superiors were asking, as well. "Your brother initially wanted us to raid the farm, but we didn't know who we were looking for and where the drugs were stashed. And Seth claimed he hadn't been privy to how the smuggling took place. At least at first. A raid too soon would have only shut down the operation here, not stopped the flow. We needed evidence. We needed facts. Still do. Seth began to gather intel and had thought he had enough to shut the ring down, but then he was killed."

Her eyes widened even more. "You really do believe he was murdered?"

"I do. Whatever information he had cost him his life." And now it put Seth's sister and nephew in danger. They weren't supposed to be here. Seth had said they lived in Washington State. And now, per Tyler's boss's mandate, Tyler and his team were to make sure the widow and her son were protected.

She shook her head. "No, *you* cost him his life. You pushed him to do something he wasn't trained to do."

The sharp tip of her barb hit him squarely in the gut. "A fact I will have to live with," Tyler stated with more regret than she could possibly know. This wasn't the first time an informant had lost his life. "But Seth got himself into this mess. Seth came to us. He knew the risks. Believe me—I wish I had done things differently."

If he could go back, he'd have extracted Seth a week ago. But Tyler had wanted more information. He'd wanted to cut off the head of the ring, not just pull in a few low-level minions. So he'd pushed Seth to keep up the pretense of going along with the drug-smuggling scheme until he knew the identity of the mastermind behind the illegal operation.

Tyler had been doing his job. A job that wasn't finished. "If I am going to bring his murderers to justice, I need to find the notebook he told me he had."

"That's why you broke into the house."

"I didn't break in. As I said, Seth gave me a key. He'd said if anything happened to him that I'd find what I needed here at the farm. I didn't mean to scare you. I had thought you and your son lived in Washington and would have returned there after Seth's burial. Otherwise I would have arranged to meet you away from the farm."

A contemplative expression crossed her face. "Ah. That's why Seth offered to pay for our plane tickets to Florida for the upcoming holiday—so we wouldn't come here." A sad light entered her eyes. "My late husband's parents live in a nursing facility there. Seth had insisted we should spend Thanksgiving with the Randalls. I declined Seth's offer." She gave a little shrug. "The Randalls barely know us, and we wouldn't be able to stay with them. I didn't want to spend the holiday in a motel."

Her words resonated with him. He spent most holidays in motels or on stakeouts. It was a lonely way to celebrate.

"And now we'll be spending the holiday here alone, without Seth."

Guilt burned at her words. He had nothing to say to soothe her hurt.

Visibly pulling herself together, she asked crisply, "What does this notebook look like?"

"I wish I knew. All Seth had told me was to get the notebook if anything happened to him." Tyler planted his feet beneath him and slowly rose. The world tilted. He swayed. He braced his feet wide, forcing back the dim shadows creeping in at the edges of his mind.

Heather rushed forward to steady him. "Take it easy. You probably have a concussion. You should go to urgent care. You might need stitches."

"I'm not going anywhere until I find what I came for." But he would lean on her for the moment, to keep from embarrassing himself again by falling flat on his face a second time. "You know how to handle a frying pan."

"If I'd had Ken's service weapon handy, I'd have used

that," she retorted drily. "But it's locked in a safety deposit box at the bank in town."

He slanted her a glance. "What were you thinking to begin with? You shouldn't have confronted an intruder. You could have been seriously wounded or killed."

From the background search he'd done on Seth and his family, Tyler knew Heather's husband had been killed in action and they had a young child, who he assumed was upstairs at this very minute unaware of the danger that could have befallen his mother.

She paled and squared her shoulders. "I had to protect my child. My husband taught me how to take care of myself. I know how to shoot a gun. I know enough self-defense to break a stranglehold. And, as you said, I know how to wield a frying pan."

He couldn't help the little burst of admiration for the gutsy lady.

Slowly she extracted herself from his side. She moved away when it became apparent he was going to stay upright.

"You're still bleeding," she said. "Come along and let me take care of your head." She turned and walked away.

He followed Heather to a large mudroom just off the kitchen, where he washed his hands while Heather grabbed a first aid kit from the cabinet over the washing machine and set it on the counter beside the washbasin. Next she dragged a chair in from the dining room.

He looked at the sturdy lattice-back chair with the pale yellow seat cushion. "I don't want to ruin any more of your cushions."

She found three towels in a drawer and brought them over. After laying one across the chair, she pushed on his shoulder. "Sit. I can't work with you standing."

Even sitting, he was as tall as her petite frame. She

stood in front of him. The scent of her skin, a mix of soap and vanilla, teased his senses. Her face was a study in concentration as she unwound the cloth she'd fastened around his head.

"This is going to hurt," she warned as she dabbed him with a cotton ball soaked in antiseptic.

The biting pain made him wince. When she finished, he sighed with relief.

"I think I can use butterfly bandages to close up the wound." She worked with quick efficiency. "Why come at night? Why not come in the daylight with a search warrant?"

"Because I didn't want to alert the bad guys that we're onto them. I was hoping to get in and out unnoticed."

She made a delicate-sounding snort. "But if you'd found the notebook, would its contents be admissible as evidence?"

"Yes, it would. The person, or persons, involved in the drug ring have no reasonable expectation of privacy on your farm, even if they are staying in one of the cabins. You're the only one who would be exempt from the rule because you're the owner. But you're not involved, so that point is moot."

"How can you be sure I'm not?"

"Seth was adamant you weren't. Plus, I did a background check on you. You're clean. I have no reason to believe you're tangled up in this mess." Could he be mistaken? His gut tightened. "You aren't, right?"

The corners of her mouth quirked, and she shook her head. "I'm not."

The last bit of doubt drained away. "Good."

"You don't even know what you're looking for," she said.

"True. But I'm sure I'll know it when I see it."

She frowned, her brow creasing. "Are you the one who called me?"

He cocked his head. "No, I never called you."

"Well, someone did, and they seemed to share your thought that Seth's death wasn't just an overdose."

A spike of concern sent his blood pressure soaring. "What did the caller say?"

"That my brother's death was more than it seemed and I should leave the farm because it's not safe."

Dread punched him in the stomach. "When was this?"

"A few hours ago."

His head pounded a rapid staccato. "All the more reason for me to find the book quickly. We need to put a stop to this fast before anyone else gets hurt."

She stepped back and put the first aid kit away, then tossed the soiled towels into the washing machine. "I'll help you look for the notebook, but first you need some fluids. Follow me."

Bemused by her take-charge attitude, he allowed her to lead him out of the mudroom. She stopped in the kitchen and turned on the light over the sink. A large butcher block served as a center island. Long wooden counters and blond oak cabinets with glass doors gave the place a homey feel. The appliances were older but clean. Blue-and-yellow gingham curtains hung over the window behind the sink. The place had a cozy feel that was foreign to Tyler.

She took a tall glass from a cupboard, filled it with tap water and handed it to him. "Drink."

"Aye, aye, Captain." He took the glass and drank the cool liquid.

She dug into a drawer and came up with two over-the-counter painkillers. "Here, these should help."

"Thanks." He popped the tablets and swallowed them with another large gulp of water. When he was finished, he set the glass on the large center island. "Let's check your brother's room."

In Seth's room they worked in silence, rummaging through drawers, checking under the mattress, under the bed. In the closet, inside the crawl space in the closet floor. Their search resulted in nothing but frustration.

Fisting his hands, Tyler glanced around the tidy room, taking in the tall dresser standing in the corner, the desk and chair placed beneath the window and the long twin bed covered in a geometric-patterned quilt.

Seth had told Tyler he'd kept the journal on the farm; it stood to reason it was in this room. There were many places to hide a notebook in the large farmhouse, but which nook or cranny had Seth used?

Tyler's head throbbed and so did his heart. He couldn't change the past, only hope he could affect the future. Wasn't that what his gran always told him?

Next they tackled the living area. It was a large great room that flowed into the dining area with the kitchen around the corner to form an L shape. Tyler searched the well-worn leather couches, while Heather checked the bookshelf, taking the books down, inspecting them and then piling them on the floor.

Tyler even checked under the large throw rug covering the hardwood in the living room. No secret compartments. No secret hiding places. He moved on to the dining room while Heather continued her slow but steady pace through the bookshelf.

The large rectangular table had no drawers or hidden slots in which to stash a notebook.

"Mommy?" A small boy stood at the bottom of the stairs staring at Tyler with wide eyes beneath a fringe of dark brown bangs. He wore footie pajamas with rockets all over them. A plush dinosaur dangled from one tiny hand.

Tyler untucked his shirt and quickly pulled it over his hip holster, hoping the boy hadn't noticed his firearm. No need to frighten the child.

"Colin, honey." Heather rushed to her son's side. "What are you doing up?"

Keeping his eyes on Tyler, the child said, "I heard a noise."

She picked him up, hugging him close. "It was just me and…" She looked at Tyler as if she weren't sure how to introduce him.

Tyler stepped closer. "I'm Tyler. A friend of your uncle Seth."

"Uncle Seth is with Daddy now," Colin replied gravely.

"Yes, he is," Tyler said. He gave the boy a sad smile. "I'm sure they are both watching over you and your mommy."

Colin scrunched up his nose. "What happened to your head?"

Heather grimaced.

"I had an accident," Tyler said, touching the bandage on his head. "With a frying pan."

Heather's eyes widened, and a pink blush stained her cheeks. He grinned at her. She flushed a deeper shade of red.

The boy snuggled into the crook of his mother's neck. She kissed the top of his head. The sight of Heather and her son made a touching picture. Tyler's chest grew tight.

"I'll be right back," Heather said and carried Colin upstairs.

Something shifted and constricted inside Tyler as he

watched them go. Heather's love for her son was obvious in the tender way she treated him. Tyler had never known that kind of love.

Certainly not from his mother. She'd been too busy scoring her next high or lost in a haze of drugs to bother with affection. Her only son had been a means to gain the weekly welfare check, nothing more.

After Heather and her son disappeared from Tyler's sight, an unfamiliar ache of longing lingered. He wasn't even sure what he longed for, but he was determined to keep Heather and her son safe.

He could only pray he didn't fail them like he had Seth.

Heather tucked Colin back into bed. "You need your sleep, big guy. Tomorrow we're helping Rob change out the village lights."

Rob Zane lived in one of the houses on the property. Her parents had offered him the job of caretaker for the farm's Christmas Village after he'd recovered from a house fire that had taken his own family nearly fifteen years earlier. A fire that some whispered he'd started. Her parents had stood by him through the arson investigation. And even though the fire had been deemed an accident, many in the area weren't convinced. He'd been kind and generous to her family in return for her parents' loyalty.

"And the decorations," Colin said, the thrum of excitement in his tone. "Rob said I could help him with Santa's house."

"That will be fun." This coming weekend they would open the farm up to the public to come enjoy the village and sleigh rides and to cut their own trees to take home. But first Heather had to get through Thanksgiving. The day wouldn't be anything like she'd hoped, but she'd do her best to make it special for Colin, despite her sorrow over her brother's death. *Murder.* She shuddered.

Careful to keep her expression from betraying the quiver of fear, she kissed Colin's forehead. "You need to get some sleep so you're bright-eyed and bushy-tailed tomorrow."

"I don't have a tail, Mommy," Colin admonished her with a grin.

She laughed, thankful for his sweet innocence, and smoothed back a lock of hair, her chest crowding with a mother's love. "No, you don't, sweetie."

Heather left Colin's room and ducked into her own bedroom to change into comfortable sweatpants and a pullover hoodie. When she went back downstairs, she found Tyler had turned off all the lights except one lamp by the couch.

He stood looking at the family photos lining the mantel with his back to her. His feet were braced apart. He had wide shoulders and a slim waist. He clenched and unclenched his hands at his sides. With anger? Frustration? Perhaps both. The bandage she'd put on his head glowed in bright contrast to his short-cropped dark hair.

Part of her was so angry with Tyler for putting Seth in danger. And yet she was angry with Seth for not telling her what was going on and getting himself involved in something so dangerous. She might have been able to help him. Or at the very least talk some sense into him.

Tyler turned around. She glimpsed the tortured expression on his handsome face before he quickly settled his features into a shuttered look that hardened the line of his jaw. She resisted the empathy flooding her veins. What did he have to be tortured about? It was her brother who'd died because Tyler and his team couldn't protect him.

Could she trust him to protect her and Colin?

What choice did she have but to put her life and that of her child into his keeping? "The only way you'll get access to the farm is if you're here on my say-so."

He narrowed his eyes. "Meaning?"

"That we do this my way."

"What's your way?"

"I'll hire you as the new foreman to take over for Seth. That way you could stay on the farm. I assume you have your team nearby. They could hire on as part of our seasonal labor." They hadn't hired enough people, and she hadn't been able to think about the shortage the past few days as she dealt first with Seth's death, then his burial.

He cocked his head to the side and appeared to consider her offer. "Only problem is I know nothing about tree farming. Anyone would see right through that."

She thought for a moment. "An investor?"

"A business partner," he countered.

"That would work. Then we'll scour the farm until we discover where my brother hid the book."

"Sounds like a great plan." Tyler held out his hand. "Partners."

After a brief hesitation—did she really want to partner with this man?—she slipped her hand into his larger one and repeated the word, answering her own question. "Partners."

His fingers curled over hers, causing a riot of sparks to shoot up her arm. Disconcerted by the odd effect of his touch, she extracted her hand. "I'll make the arrangements in the morning."

He held her gaze. "I'd appreciate it. I'll help you put the bookshelf back together."

She glanced at the stacks of books on the floor. "I'll take you up on the offer." Only because she knew she wouldn't get any sleep now anyway, not because she felt safer with him here.

Needing the calming properties of some herbal tea, she asked, "Would you like some tea?"

"Sure. I'll try some."

They moved into the kitchen. After taking two mugs from the cupboard, she dropped an herbal tea bag into each mug. Then she set the electric kettle to boil. "How are they smuggling the cocaine? And how do we stop it?"

"I don't know." Tyler leaned against the counter. "I'm confident Seth's notes will give us all the necessary details."

She poured hot water in the mugs, then slid one to him. "Hopefully this nightmare will end soon so no one else will pay the price Seth did."

Unable to continue looking at him, she stared out the window over the sink. The back of the house faced the large horse barn to the left. And farther out to the right was the processing yard where the cut trees were fed into balers and stacked, ready to be loaded onto trucks for transport.

Within the next few days, hundreds of trees would leave the farm on trucks bound for destinations all over the country and up into Canada. Not to mention all the townsfolk who would come out to take a tree home and visit the Christmas Village, eat homemade donuts, drink hot cocoa and take a sleigh ride. The busyness would take her mind off her grief. But with so many people on the property, would the danger increase?

A shadow flickered near one of the balers and stole her breath. She leaned forward, straining to see. Was she imagining the movement? She'd dismissed what she'd seen earlier as paranoia, but now...

"Heather, what is it?"

No. She hadn't imagined what she'd seen. There was definitely someone skulking around the balers. The hairs on the back of her neck rose. "Someone is out there."

THREE

Adrenaline saturated Tyler's veins at the prospect of an intruder lurking outside Heather's farmhouse. He quickly set his mug down and gripped Heather by the elbow to draw her away from the window. "Turn all the lights off and go upstairs. Don't come down until I tell you it's clear."

She blinked up at him with wide, stunned eyes. "What are you going to do?"

"Find out what's going on." Maybe this was his chance to capture those involved in the drug ring. If he could catch them in the act of hiding the drugs, then Heather and her son would be safe and he could move on to the next assignment. This one had grown exponentially more problematic. He'd rather be chasing down drug-pushing thugs than dealing with a protective mom.

He released Heather's elbow and sent her up the stairs. Once she reached the top landing, he slipped out the back door, leading with his gun in a two-handed grip. The moon provided enough light for him to navigate his way through the yard toward the three hulking pieces of machinery where Heather said she'd seen someone. He paused with his back against the side of a baler and listened.

A breeze had kicked up, and it rustled through the trees. The howl of some creature sent a shiver down Tyler's spine. Too close for his peace of mind. Had it been a wild animal Heather had seen?

Noise near the barn drew his attention. The barn's door sliding open and then closing?

He ran in a low crouch toward the large structure. Pressing his back against the side of the barn, he peered around the edge. No one there. From inside the barn, one of the draft horses used to pull the sleigh nickered. Inching his way to the barn door, he kept an eye out for any signs of life.

He eased the barn door open as soundlessly as he could. The pungent scent of hay and horse made his nose twitch. He ducked inside and hid in a pocket of shadow, waiting, listening.

A horse whinnied. The sound of metal scraping against metal raised the fine hairs on Tyler's arm. The scuff of a shoe on the dirt floor jolted through him. There was definitely someone in the barn.

Keeping low, he crept toward the rear part of the barn, where a pen had been constructed to house the smaller animals of the farm's petting zoo. He bumped into a pail, momentarily losing his balance in the dark. The noise spooked the horse to his left. Tyler reached out for the edge of the stall to steady himself just as someone bolted past him for the barn door.

"Hey!" Tyler shouted, barely making out the silhouette of a man as he yanked the door open wider and ran through.

Tyler chased after him. He caught a fleeting glimpse of the dark figure disappearing into the inky shadows of the tree crop. For a moment Tyler contempiated giving pursuit, but the prospect of getting lost among the hundreds of trees disabused him of that thought. Heather and her son needed Tyler to stand guard, in case the man decided to approach the house from another direction.

After shutting the barn door, Tyler retraced his steps to the back of the farmhouse and entered the back door. He threw the bolt into place.

"What did you see?" Heather's whispered question brought him up short. He spun around and could just barely make out her form. She stood in the archway of the kitchen, the frying pan clutched in her hands.

Achingly familiar with the damage the utensil could inflict, he kept his distance. "Someone was in the barn. They ran away when they realized I was there."

"I can't believe how paranoid I'm being," she said, laying the frying pan on the counter. "It was probably one of the farm employees checking on the barn animals. He's probably calling the police on you as we speak."

Following Heather into the living room, Tyler said, "Maybe." But he wasn't so sure. If it had been an employee who had every right to be there, why hadn't he confronted Tyler? "But you did receive a threatening phone call, right? Your paranoia is appropriate."

She blew out a breath. "You're right." She turned on a table lamp before picking up several books and arranging them in the bookcase.

"You can go on to bed and get some sleep," he told her. "I'll take care of this while I stand watch."

She made a face. "I won't get any sleep, so I might as well tackle this now."

He didn't blame her. She'd had a scary night, and there was a stranger in her house. He grabbed some books and handed them to her so she could place them on the shelf.

"Do you have a wife? Kids?"

The question punched him in the gut, stirring up an old dream that he knew would never happen for him. "No. I'm not husband material, let alone father material."

"Why would you say that?"

Aware of her curious glances, he kept his attention on the book in his hands. "I don't lead the kind of life that lends itself to settling down in one place for very long."

"Surely you must have a home somewhere."

He had an apartment where he stored his few belongings, but he wouldn't call the place homey. Not anything close to what she meant. "Los Angeles."

"Parents? Siblings?"

He arched an eyebrow. "Do you always grill your guests like this?"

She matched his arched eyebrow with one of her own. "You aren't a guest. You came uninvited into my house, my life. I think I can ask you all the questions I want."

Liking her spunk, he said, "Touché." He handed her a book. "In answer to your question, no. I'm alone in the world, and I like it that way."

He wouldn't mention that deep inside, in places he'd rather ignore, the acute emptiness of his life pressed in on him like a boulder that wouldn't budge.

Placing the last book onto the shelf, he cleared his throat and wished he could clear away his thoughts as easily. He sat in the wingback chair by the front door and stretched his legs out in front of him. "Now, if you don't mind, I'd like to get some rest."

He closed his eyes, hopefully putting an end to her curiosity. Not that he was about to sleep, not when the danger plaguing the farm could strike at any moment. On any undercover assignment or stakeout, one learned how to rest while still staying alert.

For a moment she was silent. Then he thought he heard a little huff of exasperation as she moved to the couch. A moment later the light winked out. He smiled in the dark.

Rest, my eye! Heather shifted on the leather couch. She was certain the man sitting across the darkened room had no intention of sleeping. He'd just wanted to stop her questions, which only made her more curious about him. What made a man like Tyler go into law enforcement? Why the drug enforcement agency? Why was he alone in the world?

If not for Colin, she'd be alone in the world, too.

The familiar ache of loneliness camped out in her chest. She missed her husband. Missed having someone she could count on to always have her back, to hold her when the world became too much.

In the years since his death, she'd had to learn to be strong on her own. For Colin. For herself.

Had Tyler lost someone, too? Was that the hurt she sensed in him?

The trill of her cell phone startled her. She flinched and quickly dug it out of the pocket of her sweatpants.

"Put it on speaker." Tyler's voice came to her in the dark.

Remembering the last call, she really wanted to ignore it, but burying her head in the sand wasn't smart. She needed to face this head-on. She pressed the answer button and then the speaker icon. "Hello."

"I told you once," said a muffled male voice. "You need to leave the farm. Do it now! It's not safe for you here." The caller hung up after the last word.

Alarm wormed its way through her, making her tremble.

Tyler moved to sit beside her. "Turn on the light."

With shaky hands, she groped for the switch. She turned the table lamp on and was grateful when the light dispelled the gloom.

Tyler was on his phone. "Hey, I need a call traced now." He held out his hand for her phone. She set it in his palm. He quickly rattled off her phone number to whomever was on the other side of his phone conversation. "The caller ID comes up blocked. I need to know where the call originated and if the phone can be tracked." He cupped a hand over the phone's microphone. "This will take a few minutes."

Heather drew her knees to her chest as they waited. The tick of her mother's grandfather clock sitting on the mantel seemed extraordinarily loud.

She knew the moment they had an answer by the troubled look on Tyler's face. Her blood ran cold in her veins. As soon as he hung up, she asked, "What happened? Were they able to trace the call?"

"They were able to triangulate the approximate location." He laid her phone on the couch. "The call originated from somewhere here on the farm."

Her stomach sank. Betrayal swamped her. She'd stepped into a surreal world where she had no idea what was what. Not only had her brother *not* trusted her enough to tell her what was going on, but someone on the farm wanted her gone.

"Once the guys and I have secured our covers, you and Colin should leave."

She let out a mirthless laugh. "We have nowhere else to go."

"Your in-laws?"

"I told you—they're in an assisted-living facility in Florida."

"A friend? Seth's fiancée?"

Her shoulders sagged. "My life revolves around the farm and Colin now. There's no one who I'd feel comfortable asking to stay with, especially with Thanksgiving coming up. As for Olivia, I'd rather keep her out of this. She's grieving. She doesn't need to know about Seth's troubles."

"Maybe she already knows?"

Heather shook her head. "Liv is as uptight as they come. No way would she have let Seth get away with what he was doing." She shrugged. "Besides, when I talked to her at Seth's funeral, she said she was going to visit her folks in California for the holiday."

Tyler laid his hand on her arm. "Don't worry, Heather. I'm not going to let anything happen to you or your son."

As much as she wanted to believe him, she knew that life could turn on a dime. A life, any life, could be snuffed out as quickly and as silently as a candle's flame.

The next morning dawned with a cloudless blue sky bathing the living room in soft light. Heather rubbed her stiff neck and glanced at the time on her phone. Early still. The farm employees wouldn't start their day for another couple of hours. *Good.* She needed some time to figure out how she was going to explain why she'd formed a partnership. She'd just buried her brother.

The thought brought the ache of loss to the forefront of her mind, diminishing the physical pain of stiff muscles from falling asleep sitting upright on the couch, her feet tucked beneath her. With a little start, she realized Tyler had spread the blanket that had hung on the back of the couch over her while she slept.

She was touched by Tyler's thoughtfulness, and her

gaze landed on the man sleeping in the chair across the room. After the second menacing phone call, he'd double-checked that all the windows and doors were locked. He'd taken her rolling pin and placed it into the channel of the windowsill in Seth's room, saying the window would be too easy to jimmy open.

Now his eyes were closed, his legs spread out in front of him and his arms hugged a pillow to his chest like a favored toy. For some reason the sight stirred something inside her, something she hadn't felt in a long time and refused to feel now. Not for this man. Not for any man. She'd had her one true love.

In the light of day, Tyler was even more of a presence than he'd been last night. His day's growth of beard darkened his jaw, emphasizing the contours of his face. Dark circles rimmed his eyes beneath the splay of long lashes resting against his cheeks.

Despite her anger at Agent Tyler Griffin, she appreciated that he accepted the responsibility for her brother's murder. He didn't make excuses, but he'd pushed her brother to risk his life, a means to an end. He'd put his mission before her brother's safety.

Ken had been like that. Quick to assume responsibility. Always putting the military before his family. She hated the little whisper of bitterness that floated at the edges of her mind. She'd admired Ken's dedication at first but came to resent it in time.

It had been five years since he'd left on that final mission, promising to return soon. And not a moment went by when she didn't hope there'd been some mistake and he'd come home to her and Colin.

Ken had been the love of her life. She doubted she'd ever find anyone she could love like that again. The thought filled her with a stinging emptiness.

One of Tyler's eyes popped open. Caught staring, she felt a heated flush creep up her neck. She took that as her cue to stand and divert her attention, which was hard to do considering every fiber of her being was aware of the man stirring in the chair. Plus the last thing she wanted was for him to think she was interested in him in any way.

The sooner they found Seth's journal, the quicker Tyler would be gone from her life and she could grieve in peace without worrying about drug lords and murderers.

Tyler sat up and tucked his sidearm back into its holster. He met her gaze. "G'morning."

"Morning," she replied and stretched out the kinks from the awkward position she'd maintained through the night. She went to the front window and pulled the curtains back all the way. The view of the acres of trees stretching out in all directions usually brought her a nostalgic sense of pride. This morning however, she felt only anxious.

Someone living on the farm had probably killed her brother.

And threatened her.

Who?

She clenched her fists at her sides. A sense of betrayal wrapped around her, making her pulse pound.

The quick footsteps of her son racing down the stairs forced back the tide of anger. She rounded the couch and caught him in her arms.

Lifting him high, she said, "Whoa, slow down, little man."

He stared at her with frightened eyes. "You weren't in your room."

She hugged him to her chest, sensing his unspoken fear that she, too, would go away. "I'm right here, buddy."

Colin pulled back and leaned to peer around her shoulder. "Good morning, Mr. Tyler. Are you having breakfast with us?" Colin asked.

Heather's heart hiccupped. Her son was so accepting, so trusting. She prayed he never lost that ability.

"Not today, buddy. But thank you for asking me."

Heather met Tyler's gaze. He clearly wanted to talk to her. She ruffled Colin's hair. "How about pancakes?"

Colin let out a whoop. "Pancakes!"

The second she set him on his feet, he was off at a mad dash to the dining room. The sound of a chair being dragged across the hardwood floor to the kitchen counter filled the house. A cupboard banged open. She tensed, hoping the glass bowl she imagined Colin reaching for didn't slip from his hands and break on the counter.

Tyler came to stand beside her. Her senses flared as waves of heat coming off him warmed her chilled limbs.

"I take it pancakes are a special treat?"

Tyler's low voice washed over her, making her pulse spike. Uncomfortable with her reaction to him, she stepped away. "Yes. Pancakes are a special treat."

One corner of Tyler's mouth curved upward, making him look boyish and roguish at the same time. "I'd love a rain check."

Words stuck in her throat. She nodded.

"I'm going to retrieve my truck," he said, keeping his voice low so Colin wouldn't hear him, which she appreciated. "I left it out on the shoulder of Johnstone Lane. I'll return with my colleagues Blake and Nathanial."

"Sounds like a good plan," she replied. "We'll be okay." She hoped.

"Let me program my number into your phone," he said. "Just in case. The guys aren't staying far away. We'll be back within the hour."

As she watched him punching his numbers into her phone, she had the strangest urge to plead with him not to go. She lifted her chin in determination. She would not let fear rule her life.

Tyler hesitated, suddenly loath to leave Heather and Colin, even for as long as it would take him to get his truck, go to the motel to retrieve his travel bag and the guys and then drive back here. He had a sneaking suspicion that the reason he didn't want to leave was much more complex than he wanted to admit.

This whole assignment had become extremely unpredictable. Heather and her son were distractions he couldn't afford, yet he had to stick close. To protect them.

Yeah, that was right. Wanting to stick close to the stunning widow had nothing to do with the fact he found Heather appealing.

He couldn't forget his primary objective was to bring down the drug ring and discover the identity of the mastermind. Not yearn for the dark-haired beauty.

Stalling, he found the restroom and freshened up as much as he could. But he wished he had his to-go bag handy. The stubble on his face itched. He stepped into the living room and made a decision.

Making sure his sidearm was concealed beneath his shirt, he entered the kitchen and stopped in his tracks. Colin stood on a chair pushed up to the counter. Heather was pouring milk into the measuring cup Colin held over a large bowl. The domestic scene looked like something one would see in a greeting card. Tenderness flooded his system.

"That's enough, Mommy," Colin exclaimed, then dumped the milk into the bowl.

Heather set the milk carton aside and handed him an egg. "You remember how to crack this?"

"Yes, I can do it myself," Colin insisted, snatching the egg from her hand.

Heather met Tyler's gaze over Colin's head. "Honey, I'll be right back. Try not to let any of the shells get into the mix."

Heather moved to stand in front of Tyler. She'd tied her dark hair back with a ribbon. White flour dusted her cheek. She looked so pretty and so fragile. The oversize sweats she wore hid her feminine form, but her beauty went deeper than her skin. It was in the gentle way she related to her son, in the way she'd taken care of Tyler's injury. An injury she'd inflicted out of fear and the need to protect her child.

Beneath that soft female exterior was a strong and brave woman.

"Is something the matter?"

"No, everything's good." He was quick to assure her. "I was thinking I'd have the guys pick up my truck and head on over here. If you're okay with that plan."

The relieved smile she flashed hit him square in the chest.

"Of course it's okay. That would be great. We'll make plenty of pancakes."

Fifteen minutes later, Heather's dining room was filled with three large men and one small boy who stared at the newcomers with awe as they ate pancake after pancake. She'd made a triple batch of pancake batter, fried up three pounds of bacon and made a gallon of orange juice. Though it had been years, she remembered what it was like to cook for hungry men. Ken had brought home his army buddies often to their small duplex on the Joint Base Lewis-McChord in Tacoma, Washington.

Heather didn't blame Colin for being mesmerized. She'd forgotten what it was like to be around men like these. Hard men. Men who not only faced danger but sought it out.

She'd thought Tyler intimidating on his own. Flanked by his fellow team members, she pitied anyone who would take on this trio.

US Immigration and Customs Enforcement agent Blake Fallon's hard features could cut diamonds out of stone. Though she doubted the stoic man realized how his penetrating dark gaze softened when he answered Colin's many questions in the subtle accent of the Southern states.

The other man, Canadian Customs Border Patrol agent Nathanial Longhorn, was charm personified. His comments made Colin giggle in a way usually reserved for silly cartoons. But there was a lethal grace to the man that made Heather suspect he was the type of guy one wouldn't want to cross.

"That was delicious." Tyler tilted his chair back on two legs and smiled at her across the table.

His praise brought heat to her cheeks.

"Thank you, Mrs. Randall," Blake said. His deep voice rumbled from his chest. "It's been a while since we've had a decent meal."

"Hey, now," Nathanial said. "My cooking's not that bad."

Blake raised an eyebrow. "Says you."

"You make a mean hot dog," Tyler quipped.

Heather couldn't help but laugh at the ribbing between the men.

"I will admit these pancakes were out of this world,"

Nathanial stated, then eyed Heather. "There was a touch of vanilla and something else..."

"It's a family recipe," she said. "Highly guarded."

He grinned. "Ha! A challenge. I'll ferret out the secret."

The front legs of Tyler's chair dropped to the floor. Tension radiated off him in waves as he shot to his feet. "Someone's here."

A knock at the back door punctuated his words.

Wow, how'd he know that?

"Rob!" Colin cried, jumping out of his chair and racing to the door.

"Colin, wait!" Heather hurried after him.

Nathanial snagged Colin by the waist and lifted him off his feet. "Slow up there, speedy."

Heather hadn't even seen the man rise out of his seat, let alone beat her son to the door. He carried him to the living room. Within seconds, Nathanial had her son laughing hysterically as the man acted out a story.

Tyler moved to her side while Blake disappeared from the room like a puff of smoke.

Heather frowned at Tyler. "It's Rob Zane. He's a longtime employee."

No doubt he suspected Rob was in on the drug ring, but, then again, she figured Tyler would suspect everyone on the farm.

She hated the thought that one of the farm's employees could be involved in smuggling drugs and threatening her, let alone her brother's death.

Especially the man her parents had trusted completely. She wasn't about to drag Rob into the danger surrounding the farm.

Unless he was already mixed up in it.

The thought shook her to the core.

No. She wouldn't, couldn't, believe such a thing. Despite how uncomfortable he made her feel at times, Rob was a God-fearing man. Or at least he had been once. He'd been a friend of her parents for as long as she could remember. Despite the unsubstantiated suspicions that he'd been responsible for the fire that had claimed his family, he deserved the benefit of the doubt from Heather. Didn't he?

"Heather?" Rob called, sounding worried.

"I have to answer the door," she said to Tyler. "My parents trust him."

Though his expression wasn't pleased, Tyler gave her a sharp nod. His hand rested on his holstered weapon.

Heather opened the door. "Rob, we weren't expecting you this early."

He tried to peer around her. "I wanted to make sure you were all right."

Was his concern real or a ploy to garner her trust? She stared at the man who'd become a surrogate grandfather to Colin after her parents were killed and searched for the answer to her question. In all honesty, she didn't know that much about Rob, but she had always trusted him with her son whenever they'd come home for a visit.

Now she wasn't sure who she could trust.

FOUR

"I thought I saw someone through the window, and I wanted to make sure you were all right," Rob said.

Tyler tensed, and his "something's hinky" senses went wild. Rob had been watching the house? Why?

Needing to establish his cover sooner rather than later, Tyler stepped out from behind the door. The man standing on the other side of the door was average in height and build with blond hair. He wore corduroy pants and a thick jean jacket over a black turtleneck and he leaned heavily on a cane.

Horrible scars twisted the flesh of his hands and one side of his face. Empathy crimped Tyler's gut. He'd read in the dossier about the tragedy the man had suffered, but seeing the evidence… Tyler could only imagine the agony Rob had endured, both physically and emotionally. Enough to need illegal drugs to dull the pain?

"Robbie!" Colin reentered the kitchen at a run and charged at them. Afraid the boy would bowl Rob over— he appeared unsteady on his cane—Tyler snagged Colin with one arm and lifted him to settle him on his hip. Glancing over his shoulder, Tyler saw Nathanial slip out the front door on Blake's heels.

"Mr. Tyler, this is Mr. Robbie. He takes care of the

Christmas Village." Colin patted Tyler's chest, having no idea of the turmoil he was causing inside Tyler. Holding the boy in his arms as if he were the child's parent made Tyler's heart ache in ways he'd never experienced. "Mr. Tyler's a friend of—"

"Mine," Heather interjected, cutting off her son's words. "My new business partner, to be exact."

Appreciating Heather's quick thinking, Tyler held out his hand to the other man. "Hello, Rob. I'm Tyler."

The man's shrewd gaze bounced between Tyler and Heather and back again. After a long moment, Rob grasped Tyler's hand. "Tyler, nice to meet you."

"Likewise."

"Partner?" Rob released Tyler's hand to stare at Heather.

A slight grimace pulled at the corners of her mouth. "Uh, yes."

They hadn't had time to come up with a proper explanation, so Tyler had to wing it. "I'm here to help Heather at this difficult time. More in a business advisory capacity than an operational partner."

"Ah." Obviously troubled, Rob slanted one brow upward at Heather. "I'm glad to see you're all right. Since you have company, I'll make myself scarce. When you're ready, I'll be in the village."

"Me, too!" Colin cried, launching himself toward Rob. Tyler held on fast.

"We will go to the village after you're dressed." Heather lifted Colin out of Tyler's arms and set the boy's feet on the floor. As soon as he touched down, he darted off, running through the kitchen. The echo of his feet pounding up the stairs rang through the house.

Rob's deep chuckle drew Tyler's attention.

"That child never walks. He always runs." Rob shifted on his cane with a wince.

"So I've noticed," Tyler confessed.

"We'll come help in the village a little later," Heather told Rob.

He nodded and turned to leave, but he drew up short at the sight of Blake and Nathanial standing side by side at the end of the walkway.

Tyler had to admit they made a daunting pair. Big and brawny, the two men blocked the path. Tyler cut Heather a pointed look.

Understanding widened her eyes, and she nodded. "I forgot to mention," she said, drawing Rob's attention back to her. "I hired two more hands since we're short-staffed." She motioned to the two men. "This is Blake and Nathanial."

Nathanial stepped forward and gave Rob a charming smile. "Hello. I'm Nathanial. It's nice to be working with you."

Rob shook his hand without comment.

Blake remained stoic as he shook Rob's hand. "Blake."

"Nice to meet you both," Rob murmured.

"Rob, would you show the men to the empty cabin?" Heather asked. "And then introduce them to Don." To Tyler she said, "He's our unofficial foreman now that Seth is gone." Her voice broke as she said her brother's name. Tyler felt the stab of her grief like a sharp-tipped knife to the chest.

Rob nodded. "Of course. This way." He hobbled away from the house.

Blake saluted Tyler. He inclined his head, acknowledging the agent's communication. Their undercover operation was under way.

Shutting the door, Tyler said, "I'll join the guys later."

"The cabin's barely big enough for two," she said. "I was thinking you'd be more comfortable in the carriage house. It's where we keep the sleigh. There's an upstairs apartment with running water and a kitchenette."

He'd seen the detached garage last night. Staying there would allow him to be close enough to quickly reach her and Colin if they needed him. "That would work."

Colin rushed back to the kitchen and skidded to a stop beside Tyler. "Where's Rob?"

Colin had pulled on a pair of sweatpants that were inside out and backward with the tag sticking out like a flag. He'd missed a few buttons on the plaid flannel shirt, no doubt in too much of a hurry to be careful. Tyler pressed his lips together to keep from smiling.

Heather bent down to talk to him. "He's showing Blake and Nathanial to their cabin."

"But we were going to decorate and change the light-bulbs at the village," Colin complained.

"And we will. Later." Heather rose and began clearing the table. She moved with fluid grace like a dancer. Tyler wondered if she had some training. She carried herself with an elegance that fascinated him.

Colin tugged on Tyler's hand, drawing his attention away from Heather.

"Are you coming to the village with us?" Colin craned his neck to look up at Tyler.

Swallowing back the tenderness swamping him at having the boy's hand clutching his, Tyler said, "We should help your mother clean up."

"Okay." Colin let go of his hand to grab a plate and then danced away from the dining table.

"Carefully," Heather called just as the clatter of the plate hitting the sink mocked her warning. She cringed.

"Sorry." Colin raced back to Tyler's side. "I cleaned up. Can we go now? I want to help decorate."

"There's more to do, honey," Heather said to Colin.

Needing to appease his curiosity, Tyler finally asked, "What's the Christmas Village?"

Heather smiled at Tyler as she washed a dish. "Exactly what it sounds like. We have a gift shop, bakery, a toy shop, a model train depot and, of course, Santa's house."

"And the nativity! With baby Jesus and real animals," Colin piped up as he stood on a chair to reach the empty bacon plate.

Tyler rushed to steady the chair before it tipped over. "Well, I definitely want to see this place."

There was a lot about this farm he couldn't wait to see. But, he reminded himself not for the first time, he wasn't here on a social visit. He needed to stay focused on the objective. Protect Heather and her son while finding Seth's killer and stopping the drug flow in and out of the farm. And that big Christmas Village meant lots of places to hide a journal.

Colin hopped down and took the plate to his mother.

"Did you brush your teeth?" she asked him.

He scuffed the toe in the hardwood floor. "No."

"Upstairs, buddy," Heather directed Colin. "Sixty seconds, uppers and lowers."

Colin huffed out a frustrated-sounding breath and took off like a rocket, disappearing up the staircase. It was a surprise his socked feet didn't slip out from beneath him.

Tyler picked up a towel and dried the dishes Heather set on the drain board. "So tell me about Rob." Though he'd read the dossier on the employee, he wanted to hear the man's history from Heather.

"He's been a part of our family since I was a kid. He served on the worship team at church. My mom was one of the singers on the team." She sighed, a sad sound that made Tyler's chest ache. "There was a house fire fifteen years ago. The ceiling fell on him, breaking his leg in multiple places. His wife and infant son didn't survive the flames."

Empathy twisted in Tyler's gut. "That's awful. Did they discover the cause of the fire?"

Tyler had read the police report and knew Rob was suspected of purposely starting the flames that had engulfed his house and killed his wife and son. But Tyler wanted to hear Heather's take on the tragedy.

"A plastic bag too close to a space heater. A tragic accident." She wiped her hands on a dish towel and stared out the little window over the sink.

A motor started up, though Tyler couldn't see the machinery. Outside the farm was stirring.

"He and his wife were very active in our church," Heather continued. "But after the fire he had a crisis of faith."

"It's hard to go through something like that and not wonder where God was." Tyler understood questioning God in such dire circumstances. He'd done his fair share of asking God *why* when he was a kid. Why wasn't Tyler important enough to keep his mother from using drugs? Why was he taken away from his grandparents? Why wasn't there enough food to eat?

If not for his grandparents' steadfast faith, Tyler doubted he'd have any faith now.

Heather turned to study him. "You believe in God?"

"Yes. Though it's hard at times in this line of work to not question God."

"You must see the worst in humanity."

"My fair share, anyway. But without faith, I don't know that I could do this job. I have to believe that people can be redeemed, saved from their own folly." Unfortunately, his mother hadn't wanted to give up her addiction. Not for him, not for God. "That is, if they choose to," he amended. "Not everyone does."

A thoughtful expression settled on her face. "After Rob recovered and was released from the hospital, my parents brought him to live here. He's been the caretaker of the village ever since. He likes to do something different every year so people will return. Colin's fascinated with the whole thing, just as Seth and I were as kids."

"It sounds special."

"Very special," she said. "We open for business the day after Thanksgiving. I usually look forward to the first day of the season." Her shoulders sagged. "But with Seth gone..."

She was hurting, and there was nothing Tyler could do to ease her pain except find the people responsible for her brother's death. To do that he had to find the journal. Her words sank in, and alarm bells went off in his head. "Wait a sec. You mean you still plan to open the farm for business?"

Lifting her chin, she met his gaze with a direct look. "Yes, I do. We have trees that are being harvested as we speak. There are people counting on us for their paycheck."

He shook his head. "Opening up the farm to strangers is asking for trouble."

Her eyes narrowed. "But you and your men will be here, right?"

"Yes. But that's not the point."

"Then what is the point?"

"That anyone coming or going from the farm would have access to whoever is peddling the drugs, and we'd have no way of watching every person."

"Then we both better pray you find the drugs before 9:00 a.m. on Friday morning."

Beautiful and stubborn. A potent combination. "Heather, be reasonable. Last night someone called and threatened you."

She scrunched up her nose in a cute way that distracted him for a moment. "You know, it was more of a warning than a threat. But now that you're here, Colin and I will be safe."

Tyler scrubbed a hand over his jaw. How was he going to convince her that she needed to postpone opening day of the Christmas tree farm? He understood her obligations to the employees. He weighed his options. If he shut the farm down to search for the journal, they potentially could lose the opportunity to catch the drug traffickers. If he let things unfold organically while searching covertly, then he and the guys had a better chance of apprehending the culprits.

"You have to promise me you'll be careful," he said.

Her smile was victorious. "Of course."

A chime filled the house in the tune of "Jingle Bells." Tyler cringed. "What is that?"

"The front doorbell." Heather headed for the living room.

Tyler caught her by the arm. "Another unexpected guest?"

She shrugged. "People come and go all the time."

Not liking the sound of that, Tyler took a position next to Heather out of direct sight of the door, then gave her a nod.

She opened the door and was nearly bowled over as a woman barged past her.

Tyler tucked Heather protectively behind him.

The woman stopped in the living room with her back to them and put face in her hands and sobbed. She was petite, with shoulder-length blond hair and a bright pink coat wrapped around her slight frame.

Heather skirted out from behind him to gather the other woman in her arms. Tyler got antsy looking at the two women. Was a cry fest about to ensue?

"I know, Liv," cooed Heather with a soft soothing tone. "I know."

"I just can't believe he's gone," the woman said, her voice muffled by her manicured hands.

Ah, this must be Seth's fiancée. Seth had mentioned her, saying she was the reason he stayed clean. And why he couldn't continue letting the drugs go through the farm. They were getting married, and he hadn't wanted to do anything that would jeopardize their future. Unfortunately, doing the right thing had had dire consequences for Seth. Guilt bubbled inside Tyler.

Liv's sobs subsided, and she lifted her tear-streaked face. "I'm sorry. I didn't realize how hard coming here would be."

Heather patted her shoulder. Her pretty hazel eyes darkened with sadness. "It's okay, Liv. It's hard for me, too."

Glancing around, Liv asked, "Where's Colin? I could use a hug from him."

"He's upstairs brushing his teeth."

Disappointment marched across Liv's face before she turned her dark-eyed gaze on Tyler. Something close to wariness flashed in her eyes and echoed in her voice. "Who are you?"

"A friend," Heather said before he could reply. "Tyler Griffin. This is Olivia Dorsett, Seth's fiancée."

Liv sniffled and didn't extend her hand. "Nice to meet you, Tyler." She turned to Heather and dropped her voice a little. "I didn't know you were dating anyone."

"We're not dating," Tyler said firmly. "We're business partners."

Liv's eyes widened. Was that disapproval? "I see." She dug in her purse for a tissue and blew her nose.

"Liv, why are you here?" Heather asked gently. "I thought you were going to visit your family in California."

She sniffed again. "I couldn't face all their sympathy, so I canceled the trip."

So Liv was in town? An idea formed in Tyler's mind.

Liv dug into her purse and produced a brochure. "Besides, I wanted to talk to you about a memorial service for Seth. Mr. Sanders at the mortuary recommended it as a way for people to say goodbye."

Heather paled. Her hand shook as she took the flyer from Liv. "I— That would be nice, Liv. I'm sure Seth would have liked a memorial in his honor."

"I thought so, too. I mean, the graveside service was nice and all, but so few people were there." She gave a wobbly smile. "I was thinking it would be nice to have it here in the barn. Maybe light the big Christmas tree in his honor."

"Yes. That sounds lovely. Seth loved Christmas." Heather clutched the brochure to her, crumpling the edges. "Liv, did you ever see Seth writing in a journal or notebook?"

Good question! Tyler shot an approving glance at Heather before turning his attention back to Liv.

She cocked her head to the side and frowned. "I don't recall him keeping any kind of journal or diary. Why?"

Tyler tensed. Would Heather reveal the situation to this woman? He hoped not.

"He kept one when we were kids," Heather said. "I wasn't sure if he still did. Maybe it would provide us with a clue as to why…"

Liv teared up. "As to why he overdosed. I'll look in the townhouse. He'd started moving things over in preparation. I guess I should bring his boxes back." She dug into her purse and pulled out her smartphone. She fiddled with it for a second, frowned and then said, "I've been in such a fog I forgot I have an errand to run. I should go. I'll call you later to talk more about the memorial."

"Maybe we can plan the memorial closer to Christmas," Heather said, walking toward the front door and opening it. "I don't think I can handle it emotionally right now."

Seeing an opportunity to send Heather and her son somewhere safer, Tyler gave voice to his idea. "Heather, you and Colin should go spend some time with Liv. It might be helpful for you to be together at this difficult time."

Heather shot him a sharp glance.

"Oh, normally I'd love that," Liv said quickly. "But the place is a mess. I'm a mess. It wouldn't be comfortable for you or Colin. Now, I really must go." Liv gave Heather a hug and hurried out the door.

Heather shut the door and leaned against it for a moment before straightening and squaring her shoulders. "I need to check on Colin," she said in a choked voice before she spun around and left the room.

Tyler ached for her loss and wished there was something he could do to comfort her. The only thing he had to give her was bringing her brother's murderer to justice. He went to the kitchen and poured himself more coffee, then called his boss to report in. Just as he hung up, Heather and Colin came back into the kitchen, both wearing warm coats. Heather had changed into jeans and a cream-colored cable-knit sweater.

Heather held out a shearling-lined brown corduroy jacket. Her eyes were red, no doubt from crying. But she held her chin high and regarded him with a steady gaze. He admired her fortitude. "It's brisk out, and that leather jacket of yours won't cut it. We're expecting a cold front in the next few days."

Grateful for her thoughtfulness, he took the jacket and slipped it on. It fit as if made for him. He didn't think it had been Seth's since he was shorter and stockier than Tyler. Her dad's? Or her late husband's? Mentally shrugging, he figured it didn't matter either way. He appreciated her consideration. "Thank you."

They headed out the back door. Colin ran ahead, his little legs pumping fast and his arms swinging wildly. Ah, to be that young and carefree, full of excitement for the world. Tyler couldn't remember ever being that untroubled. His youth had been spent shuffled back and forth between his mom and grandparents and sometimes even children's protective services. He'd been scared most of the time, but it had also made him tough. He could handle all that life threw at him. Yet he hoped little Colin never had to face any more hardships than what had already touched his young life.

"Not so far ahead of me, Colin," Heather called out. There was a definite tremor of concern in her tone.

Keeping his gaze on the child, Tyler said, "I'll make sure nothing happens to either of you."

She slanted him a quick glance, which he caught in his peripheral vision.

"I was thinking about getting a dog as a defense against strangers."

The not-so-subtle barb made him wince and smile at the same time. She didn't fully trust him. Not that he blamed her. He'd failed with her brother. He was determined not to fail again.

"Mommy, can I please go to the village?" Colin asked for the umpteenth time.

Heather gripped his hand, reluctant to let him roam too far from her. "We'll head there next."

They were showing Tyler the harvesting of the Douglas fir trees. The morning temperature hadn't increased much since they'd left the house. Heather tucked her free hand into her parka pocket. Her feet were beginning to ache. She wasn't used to this much walking. The job she'd left to return home had been a desk job as a receptionist for a mortgage broker. Her boots were rubbing, and her legs were tired. Showing Tyler the lay of the farm had taken longer than she'd expected because Tyler asked so many questions and wanted introductions to every worker.

Having him practically attached to her hip was wreaking havoc with her senses. Every time he bumped into her or touched his hand to her elbow, sparks shot out from the point of contact, making her face heat up. She tried to ignore the reaction, telling herself she was being silly. She was reacting to the possible danger, not to Tyler.

With each employee they encountered on the farm, she searched for some clue to indicate malicious intent. But try as she might to find something or someone suspicious, she only found the same people who had worked for the Larson tree farm every holiday season for years.

Though she had moved away at age eighteen, she'd always returned for opening weekend. She knew and trusted these people. Or she had trusted them until yesterday when the world she'd thought she'd known went spinning out of control like a child's toy top by the appearance of the man standing at her side.

She amended that thought. It wasn't fair to blame everything on Tyler. Her brother had started this mess by allowing a drug cartel to use their family's farm to move illegal narcotics. Every time she thought about what Seth had done and the danger he'd put himself and everyone else in, anger flooded her system until she thought she might drown. Seth had made so many impulsive, irresponsible decisions in his life. And his last one had been a whopper.

A choice that had rippling consequences.

Not only had Seth been murdered; now she and Colin were potentially in danger.

And the only defense she and her son had were three men, albeit well-trained ones. She sent up a silent prayer that Tyler and his IBETs colleagues would be enough to keep her and her son safe.

They stopped near a flatbed truck loaded down with a mound of trees that had been through the baler, a machine that wrapped the trees in twine so they could be more easily transported. The trees were then stacked and chained in place.

Colin broke free and ran a few paces away. He squatted down to poke at something on the ground. "Mommy, it's a roly-poly bug."

She smiled, thankful he still found things like bugs interesting. "Don't squish it."

His brows puckered. "I wouldn't do that!"

"Are all the trees transported like this?" Tyler asked, studying the flatbed, drawing her attention away from her son.

"When the delivery location is within the state." Gesturing to the larger refrigerated box trucks a few yards away, she said, "These trucks are used for longer hauls to other states—and into Canada." A lightbulb went off in her head. "Do you think the drugs were smuggled in these vehicles?"

"I was wondering the same thing," Tyler said with a speculative gleam in his eyes. "Have you ever been inside one of these trucks?"

'No, I've never had a reason to. Seth handled all of that."

"I think I need to inspect these trucks," Tyler said.

Before she could respond, the loud rattle of a chain releasing from its mooring rent the air.

"Watch out!" someone cried.

FIVE

Heather had no time to process the sharp cry of warning before a hard body rammed into her, lifting her off the ground, sending them both flying out of the path of an avalanche of trees spilling from the flatbed and landing in the spot where she had just stood.

Heart hammering, Heather scrambled to her knees, her gaze going to the mound of trees. Her mouth dropped open. She could have been crushed.

"Are you okay?" Tyler gripped her by the shoulders, forcing her to look at him. His bright blue eyes were filled with anxiety. "Did I hurt you?"

He'd tackled her to prevent her from being flattened by the trees. He'd saved her life.

Colin!

Her attention whipped to her son. He sat a few feet away with his arms wrapped around his knees, his eyes round.

"Heather?" Tyler persisted.

She put a hand on Tyler's arm. "I'm okay thanks to your quick reaction." Gratitude flooded her. He'd acted swiftly, without thought to himself. That kind of selfless act touched her deeply and dissolved any lingering anger.

He nodded, expression grim. He helped her to her feet. Colin jumped up and ran to her, colliding with her legs and nearly knocking her back to the ground. His arms wrapped around her and held on tight. Her heart swelled with love for her son.

"You two stay put while I figure out what happened." Tyler went to the truck to inspect the chains that had held the trees in place.

Heather gathered Colin in her arms. He clung to her, putting his head on her shoulder. She hugged him, savoring the moment while her pulse still zinged at a rapid clip.

A dozen men crowded around them, asking if they were hurt. Suddenly feeling vulnerable and claustrophobic with so many people pressing in on her and Colin, Heather said, "Please, everyone, we're okay. Give us some breathing room."

"Come on, guys, let's give Mrs. Randall space," said Don Kline. Don was one of the farm's longest-employed workers. He had been the unofficial foreman since Seth's death. Don was in his late sixties with a shock of white hair and wide girth that made him the perfect choice to play Santa during the holiday season. He wore navy coveralls, work boots and thick gloves and a worried scowl on his weathered face.

Heather grasped his offered hand. The work gloves were rough against her palm as he drew her and Colin farther away from the scene of the accident.

"Mommy, Mr. Tyler saved you." Awe filled Colin's voice.

She patted his back while her gaze sought out Tyler. He and Blake were conferring near the trailer bed. Tenderness choked her. "Yes. Yes, he did, honey."

She thanked God above for Tyler's quick action.

If he hadn't reacted as quickly as he had, she'd have been seriously injured or killed. A quiver of fear raced through her. Had it been an accident? Or something more sinister?

Tyler joined them. "Someone cut the chain holding the trees in place."

Alarm tightened Heather's neck muscles. Someone deliberately tried to hurt her? *No.* That couldn't be.

There was no way anyone could have predicted she'd be standing in that spot at that exact moment. But then why would someone sabotage the flatbed's chain in the first place?

She tried to remember who had been standing on the other side of the truck from her. But she hadn't noticed. Her focus had been on Tyler, on the connection sparking between them. Further proof of how foolish it would be for her to allow him past her defenses. She'd almost been killed by her inattention. And if Colin had been standing there… She shuddered.

Don frowned. "Are you sure? Why would someone do that?"

Tyler placed his arm around Heather. This time she edged closer to him, grateful for his steady presence. "Have you had any other trouble on the farm?"

Don's bushy white eyebrows twitched. "No, not really. Well, other than poor Seth's death."

The reminder of her brother's murder made her hug Colin tighter.

Tension radiated off Tyler, adding to her already tightly strung nerves.

"What do you mean by 'not really'?" Tyler asked. "Has something else happened?"

Don rubbed a hand over his jaw. "Earlier this month

we had a shipment of fertilizer go missing. That's never happened in the nearly forty years I've been here."

Tyler's fingers flexed against her shoulder where his hand rested. "How much fertilizer are we talking about?"

"Four hundred pounds." He waved his hand toward the acres of small, medium-size and large trees. "We have a great deal of ground to cover."

"That's not good." She watched news reports on the television; she knew fertilizer was a component used to make bombs. Her stomach roiled. She shifted Colin to the side. "Why didn't I know about this?"

Don grimaced. "Seth said he'd take care of it. Another order appeared within a few days. I assumed it had been some sort of mix-up."

Her stomach dropped. Had Seth provided some terrorist faction with the means to create an explosive device? *Oh, Seth, what were you thinking?*

Tyler nudged her. "I need to make a phone call."

A cold numbness washed over her as they walked back toward the farmhouse. As soon as they were far enough out of hearing distance of the employees, Tyler paused and withdrew his cell phone from his cargo pants.

Heather strode away with Colin, not wanting him to hear the details of Tyler's call. Undoubtedly, he was calling his boss or some other law enforcement person who dealt with terrorists and bombs. She shivered and set Colin down. Holding on to his hand, she pointed out the different types of trees.

"I know, Mommy," he said. "Uncle Seth explained that each has its own uniqueness."

"Did he?" She was glad Colin would have good

memories of her brother. "Did he tell you that he and I helped plant most of the trees?"

"Uncle Seth said for every tree that is cut down, we replant two."

"That's right. And see on this stump how there's still a live branch? In twenty years, the tree will have grown and be ready to harvest again. We have to be good stewards of the gifts God has given us." This land, this farm, was her family's legacy. She had to protect it for her son.

Tyler walked over. His troubled expression didn't bode well. "I informed my boss," he whispered. "ATF will look into the missing fertilizer."

"Will more agents arrive, wanting access to the farm?" she whispered back.

"Not unless they have intel that can link the farm to a terrorist cell." She wasn't sure if she was relieved or more terrified.

"It's not polite to whisper," Colin scolded them with a scowl.

Heather bit back a surprised laugh. "You're right, honey. It's not. But sometimes grown-ups have to talk about issues that aren't meant for little boys."

His face brightened. "Like my Christmas present?"

This time the laugh escaped. "Definitely like Christmas presents."

"That's not just for adults," Colin said. "Uncle Seth and I whispered about your present."

Her pulse accelerated. She shared a startled glance with Tyler. "What is it?"

Colin tsked. "I can't tell you, Mommy. It's a surprise."

Tyler hooked his thumbs into his belt loops. "You can tell me. I'm really good at keeping secrets."

Colin's face scrunched up as he debated. Finally, he nodded and crooked his finger at Tyler. Tyler knelt down so that Colin could whisper in his ear. The dark shade of their hair was so close in color it was hard to distinguish where one stopped and the other started.

Heather held her breath as an ache deep inside came to life. Seeing them together like that brought home how much Colin was missing out on by not having a father in his life.

She had to be both mother and dad. The load of responsibility weighed heavily on her shoulders, but she gladly, and lovingly, bore the burden. She would do whatever it took to make sure her son grew into a responsible, worthwhile man.

When Colin was done, he stepped back with a grin.

"Well done," Tyler said and high-fived her son before standing.

Dying of curiosity, Heather stared at Tyler, willing him to spill the beans. Anticipation tensed her shoulder muscles and chased away the numbness. What had Seth left her? Could it be the journal?

He winked. "It's a good present. Perfect for a six-year-old to give his mother."

She let out a breath as the tension left her body. Obviously not Seth's journal. "I'll have to wait for Christmas morning, then."

"Are we ready to see the Christmas Village?" Tyler asked.

"Yeah!" Colin jumped up and down and clapped his hands.

Tyler's deep chuckle caught Heather off guard. The sound was rich and warm and something she wanted to hear again.

"Lead the way, little buddy," Tyler said.

Colin raced away.

"Hey! No!" Concern arched through her.

Tyler caught her hand in his. "Come on, Mom. We have to catch up."

Stunned, it took a second to comprehend what he meant, and then he tugged on her hand and she had no choice but to break into a jog to maintain pace with him. They had to increase their combined speed to keep Colin in sight. It felt good to move, to exercise her legs, her lungs and her heart. As if running could distance her from the mess her brother had left behind.

The cool air swept over her face, ruffling her hair and making her feel alive in a way she hadn't in a long while. By the time they made it to the other side of the property where the Christmas Village sat off the main highway, giving the public easy access to the wide gravel parking lot, she was winded but exhilarated, as well.

Seeing the village stirred a nostalgic sense of well-being. She'd loved this place as a kid. Who was she kidding? She still did, even with danger looming over her like a gloomy cloud.

A high arch structure built by her great-grandfather marked the entrance to the village. Fresh green garland snaked around the arch. Embedded in the greenery were tiny white lights. A big gold satin bow with long tails graced the top of the arch.

Inside the village, constructed to replicate an Old West town, employees worked to prepare for opening day. The various storefront facades were in varying stages of decorating with gold ribbons, gold ornaments of different sizes and gold garland mixed with greenery around the wood railing of the ramps that allowed for wheelchair access.

It seemed this year Rob was going for a golden Christmas theme. She couldn't wait to see what he did with the sleigh. Would he paint it gold? She remembered one year when he'd done a white-and-blue Christmas theme, he'd painted the sleigh blue and hung white lights on it.

Coming to a halt, Heather put her hand over her racing heart. "I haven't run that far in ages."

Tyler grinned, knocking what little breath remained in her lungs out with a one-two punch.

"Whew!" Tyler said. "Is your son training for a long-distance race?"

Catching her breath, she forced her attention to where Colin was talking with Rob outside the bakery shop. "He has a lot of energy—that's for sure."

"He's a good kid."

"Thank you."

"You're a good mom. It shows in Colin."

His comment raised her curiosity. "Have you had much experience with kids?"

He let out a small scoffing laugh. "Not to speak of. But I've seen enough unruly children in public places to spot a genuinely well-behaved kid when I see one. And I would hazard a guess that has a great deal to do with parenting."

"The old nurture versus nature debate, huh?"

"I don't know. But I have to believe that having a parent who loves and cares for their child the way you do Colin, that he's bound to turn out well."

"You must have had good parents, then," she said. "You turned out well."

He blanched. "No. I didn't."

Did he mean he didn't have good parents or that he hadn't turned out well? Or both?

Did she really want to know? Somehow, getting close enough for him to share his history with her scared her. She wasn't looking to get emotionally involved with this man. He was here for a purpose. And it wasn't to comfort her lonely heart. It was to protect her and her son's life. And bust a drug ring. She would do well to remember that despite how much the thought of comfort from him appealed to her. She shoved her hands into the pockets of her red parka.

She had to stop this nonsense and focus on her priority. Her son. "I believe that having a relationship with God is what makes the difference. He is, after all, the ultimate Father."

One side of his mouth slanted upward. "You're right."

They joined Rob and Colin. The delicious aroma of cinnamon and vanilla wafted out of the bakery building. Heather's mouth watered. "Ohhh, Mrs. Theid is making sweet rolls."

"Can I get one?" Colin danced on his toes.

"Me, too," Tyler said, giving Colin another high five.

Amusement danced in Rob's eyes. "I told Colin he'd have to ask you."

Colin and Tyler both gave her a beseeching smile that melted her insides like warm butter on a sweet roll. "Pastries for lunch?"

"Pleeeeeease," Colin said with a wide smile that showed all his little teeth.

Rob chuckled. "How can you resist that face?"

"Right," Tyler chimed in with a big toothy grin of his own. "How can you resist?"

Unable to deny them the treat, she relented with a laugh. "All right. But we've got to head back to the house for some real lunch. A healthy lunch."

"Aww, we just got here," Colin protested.

"Let's not push it, buddy," Tyler said, holding out his hand to Colin. "Let's get a treat." He looked at Heather expectantly. "You coming?"

"I'll be right there," she assured him. "Mrs. Theid was one of my mother's best friends. I should come in and say hello." But she didn't move. Maybe it was because the thought of going inside the bakery with Tyler and Colin as if they were a family unit left her mouth dry and tore a chunk out of her heart.

Tyler hesitated, clearly torn between wanting to stay close to her and wanting to fulfill his word to her son. Tyler was a good man. She'd only had a few hours on which to base her assessment, but so far he'd proven he was a man of honor and integrity. A man worth taking a second look at. But she wasn't looking, not once, not twice.

Colin tugged on his hand, practically dragging Tyler through the bakery door.

Seeing the two walking into the shop hand in hand made her insides melt all over again. She wished she could bottle up this time and keep it for darker days when she and Colin needed a little pick-me-up.

"He seems like a decent guy," Rob said, reminding her she wasn't alone.

"Yes. He does."

And that was a problem.

One she didn't know how to solve. But it was clear she was going to have to guard her heart if she hoped to get through this unscathed. She'd lost her one true love. She had no intention of putting herself at risk again.

Shifting her focus to the village decorations, she said, "Gold this year. I like it."

"It seemed appropriate since this is the golden anniversary of the farm's Christmas Village."

A fist-size knot tightened in her chest. Of course it was. If she'd been paying attention, she'd have remembered. Every Christmas season her parents had been marking off the countdown to the anniversary. Her great-grandparents had bought the farm nearly eighty years ago but waited until their own children were grown and had their own lives before building the village and opening it up to the public.

Touched by his observance of the date, she said with honest gratitude, "Thank you, Rob, for remembering."

"Of course. You are very important to me."

Swallowing back the unease itching its way up her throat, she replied, "Our family is grateful for all you do."

She stared at his scarred face, battling the suspicions rearing within her mind. Was he involved with the drug smuggling? Or was he innocent?

Seth had looked to Rob as a surrogate father. Did she dare take a chance on asking Rob about the journal? Would she be tipping off the bad guys? Where had Rob been standing when the chain on the trees let loose? Had Rob been involved with Seth's death? Was Colin safe with Rob around? Colin looked up to Rob. It would tear him up to discover the man was in any way responsible for Seth's death. And her parents had trusted him...

She looked away from Rob to gaze over the village. She recognized every face. Year after year these same people journeyed to the tree farm to help make Christmas bright for others. Yes, they were paid, but each one enjoyed their time here enough to return. She'd never worried about her or Colin's safety here on the farm before. But now she stared at each person and questioned whether they were really what they seemed. Any one of these employees could be involved in the drug-smuggling ring. Involved in Seth's death.

A throbbing headache pounded behind her eyes, and

her stomach burned with agitation. She didn't know how long she could handle the dread that seemed to have taken up residence inside her. She prayed it wouldn't have to be long and that she and Colin would make it through alive. With their hearts intact.

The cute little bakery was bigger on the inside than Tyler had expected with a full kitchen, large ovens, a few tables and chairs. And the most decadent-looking array of pastries and candies Tyler had seen in a long time.

Before they were served, he called Nathanial and asked him to bring the truck around. Tyler didn't think any of them were up for the hike back.

The woman behind the counter, Mrs. Theid, boasted that all her treats were homemade. She'd been working for the Larsons since before she was married, and she'd just celebrated her thirty-third anniversary.

Tyler hadn't been free to ask too many questions with Colin next to him. But what he did learn made him realize there were more people involved in the Larson Christmas tree farm than he'd first thought. Which meant more suspects to cull through.

Tyler followed Colin out of the bakery, their hands filled with large gooey sweet rolls dripping with icing. One look at Heather's face had concern crowding out his enjoyment of the pastry in his hand. He cocked his head as he studied Heather. Her face had lost some of the color she'd had from their run. And her lips where pressed tightly together, her eyes troubled. "You okay?"

Her smile looked forced. "Yes. Though I'd like to head back now. I'm tired."

"I called Nathanial and asked him to bring my truck around to pick us up."

"You did?" Heather's eyes brightened. "That was thoughtful of you."

As if on cue, a horn honked. Nathanial waved from the driver's seat of Tyler's large black truck with an extended cab.

Colin's face scrunched up, but Heather held up a hand before he could protest. "We will return to help later. I promise."

Colin huffed and then chomped on the roll, apparently satisfied with her words. Tyler liked that she was firm yet kind with the boy. So different from the way his mother and his grandparents had treated him. He'd dealt with both extremes. His mother had been harsh, sometimes mean when she was coming down off a high, whereas his grandparents had been overindulgent with their affection and praise.

They climbed into the cab of the truck.

"You didn't bring me one of those?" Nathanial groused good-naturedly, eyeing the remnants of their pastries.

"Wouldn't want to ruin your figure," Tyler shot back, then finished off his pastries with a flourish.

Nathanial grinned as he drove. "You got that right. Too bad you can't say the same for yourself."

Tyler chuckled. He liked the Canadian. They'd only worked together a handful of times, but Tyler could count on Nathanial to have his back.

Glancing over his shoulder at Heather, who stared out the side window with a pensive look on her face, Tyler wondered what Rob had said to upset her. He still hadn't made up his mind about Rob. He seemed to genuinely care for Heather and Colin, but there was something off with the guy. And that bugged Tyler.

When they reached the house, Tyler climbed out and

opened the rear cab door for Heather. Nathanial did the same for Colin.

"I need a moment with Nathanial," he told Heather as she climbed out. "You and Colin wait for me on the porch, okay?"

She nodded, but he wasn't sure she really heard him. He snagged her elbow. "What's wrong?"

Her brows knit together. "Everything. I hate this. I hate not trusting the people working on the farm. I hate the fear that something bad will happen to me or Colin."

Hurting for her, he brushed back strands of dark hair that clung to her cheek. "I know. I wish you weren't going through this. But we'll get to the bottom of this—I promise."

For a long moment she stared at him, her eyes so forlorn and vulnerable. He fought the need to take her in his arms and assure her all would be well. But he didn't. Couldn't. Letting this assignment become any more personal than it already had was a bad idea.

His boss had commanded him to stick close to the widow and her son, to protect them. Not so he could fall for the beautiful lady and her adorable kid. He ignored the little whisper inside his head that told him he was fast on his way to falling and there wasn't a safety net to catch him.

Man, he needed to get his head in the game and out of the clouds. There was no possible future in letting himself become emotionally attached to this woman.

Yet, holding her gaze, with the strong pull of attraction weakening his resolve, he found all he wanted to do was gather her to him and kiss her.

The sound of Colin's feet pounding up the porch stairs broke through the moment. He stepped back, thankful for the reprieve. "I need to talk to Nathanial."

She nodded and walked away.

Forcing himself to not watch her, Tyler came around the front of the truck to where Nathanial leaned against the grill.

"We have a problem," Tyler told Nathanial. "There are more employees—"

"Tyler!"

Heather's frantic cry from inside the house sent Tyler's pulse skittering.

SIX

Heart flooding with adrenaline, Tyler raced inside the Larson farmhouse with his hand on his weapon and a prayer on his lips. He had asked Heather to stay on the porch and wait for him, but she'd gone ahead and entered the house unaccompanied.

He shouldn't have let her get out of arm's reach. That was unprofessional and plain stupid. If she ended up hurt because he'd made an error, he'd never forgive himself. He already carried enough guilt for not having extracted Seth before his duplicity was discovered.

Tyler raced into the living room, while Nathanial hurried past him to clear the kitchen. The place had been ransacked. Tyler surveyed the destruction for half a second. The books they had painstakingly gone through the night before and arranged on the shelves were now littering the floor in a haphazard fashion. Throw rugs had been lifted and carelessly deposited in a heap in the corner. Couch cushions had been slashed, the stuffing spilling out. The side tables turned over. The lamp smashed.

"Heather!"

"Here." Her voice came from down the hallway on the ground floor.

He rushed to her side outside her brother's room. She held Colin in her arms, his face buried in her neck. "Are you hurt?"

She shook her head but shock clouded her eyes. "Someone…"

He followed her gaze into Seth's bedroom. Here the damage was more vicious. The dresser had been toppled. The mattress pulled from the frame. The floorboards ripped up. Clothes stripped off the hangers and shredded. The senselessness of the carnage appeared personal, as if the perpetrators had been taking out their aggression on Seth's belongings.

Gripping her elbow, Tyler led Heather back to the living room. They met Nathanial at the bottom of the stairs.

"The kitchen and the rooms upstairs have been searched," Nathanial said in a tone filled with anger.

Colin whispered something into Heather's ear. She nodded and set him down. He ran to the bathroom and shut the door behind him.

"Do you think whoever did this was looking for the journal?" Heather asked.

"I think that's exactly what it means." Tyler had to admit he hoped that the extent of the ransacking was a sign the bad guys didn't have the notebook. But it also meant Seth's murderer knew about the records he was keeping. "When we searched we didn't see any signs of loose boards or hidden compartments in the furniture."

"I wish Seth had told you exactly where he'd hidden the notebook," Heather said in a strained voice. "It could be anywhere on the farm."

Tyler didn't like hearing the miserable tone. He wouldn't let her give up. "And we will find it."

"I hope so," she said with a weary sigh. "We need to call the police."

Tyler exchanged a glance with Nathanial. "Bringing in local law enforcement could jeopardize our investigation by spooking the people we're trying to catch."

Heather arched an eyebrow. "Won't it seem suspicious if I don't call the police? We know whoever did this is working for or with the drug cartel and is probably keeping an eye on me and the house. If the police never show, they'll know and wonder why not."

"True. We need to act as if we aren't aware of the drug ring." Tyler took out his phone and called the Bonners Ferry sheriff's department. They promised a deputy would be out to take their statements for a report.

Tyler knew the procedure. They would take print samples and look for trace evidence. All standard and necessary. However, Tyler held little hope that the perp would leave behind anything incriminating. Not when they'd been so careful committing Seth's murder and making it look like an accidental overdose.

"I need to make sure nothing of value was taken," Heather said as Colin came out of the bathroom and clung to her leg, his eyes wide.

Kneeling down so he could be at eye level with Colin, Tyler said, "I know you're scared, but I won't let anything bad happen to you." So many bad things had happened to them already. Tyler would do everything he could to make her and Colin's world better. Safer. He gestured to the living room and the damage. "This can all be fixed."

Colin straightened. "I'll help."

Tyler put his hand on the boy's thin shoulder. "You can certainly help once the police have done their thing."

They waited out front for the sheriff's deputy to arrive. As it turned out, Sheriff Paul Rodriguez came out to the farm along with a crime scene unit. He took their statements and waited while Tyler and Colin helped her straighten up the mess left by the intruder. She'd found nothing of value missing.

The sheriff pulled Tyler aside. "I've spoken with your boss, Agent Griffin. If there's anything the Boundary County sheriff's office can do to assist in your investigation, you let us know."

"Thank you, sir." Tyler shook his head. "I appreciate the offer." And he was surprised. He was glad the situation hadn't turned into a turf war. Sometimes the local law got a bit prickly when any of the federal agencies came into their territory working a case.

After the sheriff and the crime scene unit left, Tyler crouched next to Colin. "Let's get that healthy lunch your mother was talking about so we have fuel in our bellies to get the job done."

With a solemnness that tore at Tyler's heart, Colin nodded and tugged on Heather's hand. "Come on, Mommy. We need fuel."

Tyler rose. The gratitude in Heather's hazel eyes gripped him by the throat. She smiled and mouthed, *Thank you.*

Forcing himself to stay on task, he turned to Nathanial and gestured toward the living room. "Can you deal with this?"

"Yep. Nothing a little duct tape can't fix," Nathanial said. "I have some in my to-go bag."

Not taking the time to ask the Canadian why he traveled with duct tape, Tyler ushered mother and son into the kitchen. Drawers had been removed from their railings; cupboard doors were open and the shelves empty.

Dishes were knocked haphazardly on the counter and floor. Fortunately, several had escaped damage.

Without comment, Heather picked up the silverware drawer and threaded the roller on the slide frame to put the drawer back into place. Tyler caught Colin's eye and pointed to the pots on the floor. The boy immediately replaced the pots and pans to their rightful cabinet, while Tyler tackled putting the dishes in their proper place. Once the kitchen was in working order, Heather shooed Tyler from the room.

"Go help Nathanial," she said. "Colin and I have this."

Sensing her need for space, he agreed. "I'll be in the next room if you need anything."

She smiled her thanks, but her eyes glittered suspiciously. Struggling to maintain his focus and pushing back the urge to pull her into his arms, he turned and left the kitchen.

He joined Nathanial in the living room. He was working on restuffing the couch cushions and securing the insides with long strips of silver duct tape.

"The lady okay?" Nathanial asked.

Tyler gathered books and replaced them on the bookshelf. "Rattled."

"The good news is, whoever did this won't be looking here again," Nathanial stated. "The bad news is they will be looking elsewhere on the farm."

"We have to get to Seth Larson's notebook before they do." Tyler's fingers flexed around the thick book in his hand. "I wish I knew who 'they' were. The farm employs nearly a hundred people, way more than I originally estimated."

"We start taking names and running them." Nathanial righted an end table and lamp. "Something will pop."

Finished with the bookshelves, Tyler repositioned the throw rugs on the hardwood floor. "We need to search the grounds. How many cabins are there?"

"I counted six plus another small house where the tightlipped Rob lives."

"It might be worth checking that the cabins and Rob's place haven't suffered the same fate as the farmhouse."

"Right." Nathanial tipped his chin. "You got this?"

"I've got this." Tyler would put everything back in place, sure. But he wouldn't be able to make this right for Heather until they found that journal. Everything rested on the notebook Seth had hidden. Where was it? And why were the bad guys one step ahead of him? If he failed to catch them…

The fear of failing Heather burrowed in deep, making him even more determined to protect her and her son.

Later that evening, after restoring Colin's room to its original form, Heather put Colin down to bed earlier than usual. The day had taken an emotional toll on them both.

She was thankful her bedroom hadn't suffered the same degree of assault that Seth's room had. Had the intruder assumed Seth wouldn't hide the journal where Heather might stumble upon it? The thought that whoever had done this knew her family so well made her skin crawl.

She'd had to bag up Seth's ruined clothes. No sense in putting them back in the drawers or on the hangers in the closet. Thankfully the bedding had been spared.

The living room looked almost normal. She'd have to replace the lamp, but that was easy enough. The cushions now had duct tape on one side. She appreciated the men's attempt to patch things together. But nothing could change the fact that her brother was dead and bad people were roaming her family's farm.

After kissing Colin good-night, she headed downstairs. Tyler sat at the kitchen table with a laptop and a printed list of the farm's employees he'd obtained from Payroll, which she'd given him access to. She stood in the shadows, watching him work. His broad shoulders were hunched, his fingers pecked at the keys and his focus darted back and forth between the computer screen and the list of names on the sheets of paper at his side.

Two days' worth of stubble darkened the contours of his strong jaw. The planes and angles of his face were deepened by the play of light from the drop-down light fixture hanging over his head. It was strange to have him in her house, underfoot. Despite the chaos of her home being ransacked and the stress of knowing someone on the farm had killed her brother and was using the farm to peddle drugs, she had every faith that Tyler would keep her and Colin safe. He had a way of making them both feel cared for.

But Tyler was only here temporarily. She would do well to remember that. Soon he would be gone, and her life would return to…what it was before he'd shown up. She could hardly remember what that felt like despite it being less than twenty-four hours ago. She had to guard against letting Tyler break into her heart.

He glanced up and smiled, knocking the breath from her lungs. "Colin settled in for the night?"

She was glad he couldn't see the heat in her cheeks. "For now." With a deep breath, she pulled back the attraction zinging through her blood and walked briskly into the kitchen. "I'm making tea. Would you like some? Or would you rather have coffee?"

"Coffee, thank you." Tyler rose and stretched to his full height. Heather was momentarily dazed as she watched, appreciating his trim muscular frame. When he moved to lean against the kitchen counter, she quickly busied herself with the coffeemaker and the electric kettle.

"How are you doing?" he asked.

Her first thought was to prevaricate. Tell him she was just dandy. But she was far from all right. She was freaked out by the danger, attracted like crazy to him and totally irritated by the circumstances she'd found herself in.

All control of her life seemed to have run out the door. She was on the edge and not sure how much more she could take. But she had to hold it together. *Be strong.* Colin needed her to be strong. "I'm hanging in there."

Needing to redirect his interest away from her, she asked, "Have you made any discoveries?" He'd told her he wanted to check the employees against the National Crime Information Center's database.

"So far I'm not finding anything to indicate who might be working with the drug cartel."

"That's good, I guess." She set the kettle to boil for her tea, then readied a coffee mug. "If I hadn't received that phone call and someone hadn't trashed my house, I would question whether or not Seth had really helped smuggle drugs using our farm. We saw no sign of drugs today. And I'm assuming your men didn't either."

"No, they didn't. But that doesn't mean anything. It's been my experience that those in the drug trade are crafty. They know how to hide their stash from even experienced agents."

"What about dogs?" She grabbed two mugs from the cupboard and dropped an herbal teabag in one. "Couldn't you bring in a K-9 unit to sniff out the narcotics?"

"We could and may if we don't find anything soon. But once we do that, our cover will be blown and we can kiss any chance of shutting the pipeline down goodbye."

"And you won't settle for the minions," she said, remembering what he'd said the night before. She poured hot water into her mug. "You want the head bad guy."

He inclined his head. "That's the goal."

She admired his dedication even as she prayed his quest to take down the drug cartel didn't harm her or her son. She prepared his coffee and slid the cup to him. "How long have you been with the DEA?"

"Eight years." His hand wrapped around the hot mug. "I applied to become an agent right out of college."

He'd started out young. "Did you always want to go into law enforcement?"

"Yes." He sipped the black liquid, apparently impervious to the heat causing steam to rise in the cool air.

She waited, using her own heated mug to warm her hands. When he didn't elaborate, she asked, "What drew you to the drug enforcement agency?"

He stared into his cup. For a long moment, he was silent.

She told herself to stop pressing. Learning more about him may appease her curiosity, but it would also endear him to her even more than he already was, and that wasn't a good plan.

"My mom was an addict," he finally confessed. "The drugs killed her."

"I'm so sorry."

No wonder he'd followed the path he had. His relentless pursuit of those who imported and exported the poison that had destroyed his mother made sense now. And it formed a bond between them. One she couldn't undo with the knowledge that drove him. They both had lost people they loved. She'd lost Seth to drugs, just as Tyler had lost his mother. But bonds of grief weren't enough to build a future on, not that she was looking to build anything with Tyler.

He shrugged. "Nothing for you to be sorry about."

His nonchalance didn't fool her. She knew the heart-ache of watching someone battle an addiction. And lose. As much as Seth had wanted to be clean and stay clean, he'd still found a way to let drugs kill him. "How about your father?"

He gave her a rueful smile. "Don't know him. Mom never said who he was, and when I asked, she'd get mad so I stopped asking. Even my grandparents didn't know who he was."

Empathy gripped her heart again. That had to be tough on a boy. At least Colin knew his father had loved him and had died a hero.

Tyler was a hero, too. He was driven by a need to rid the world of the drugs that had robbed him of his mom. Just as drugs had robbed her of Seth.

The flash of headlights sweeping across the kitchen window sent a jolt through her system. She wasn't ex-pecting anyone at this late an hour.

Tyler set his mug down. With a hand on the weapon at his side, he moved to the kitchen door and looked out the window. "It's Liv." He hid his sidearm beneath his black T-shirt.

Surprised Olivia had returned, Heather moved to open the door as Liv stepped up to knock. Liv's gaze widened slightly when she saw Tyler. He moved to the dining table to close his laptop and gathered the papers to stuff into his leather backpack.

Unmistakable curiosity gleamed in Liv's eyes. "I'm sorry, is this a bad time?"

"No," Heather said. "Not at all. Come in."

Liv had changed into black leggings tucked inside tall black boots. She slipped out of her classy black-and-white houndstooth wool coat. Beneath she had on a knee-length sheath dress. She looked elegant and smart. Heather wished she'd changed out of her grubby jeans and sweater into something more… She mentally snorted. *Stop it.* It didn't matter how she looked. She wasn't trying to gain anyone's attention, and she certainly couldn't compete with Liv when it came to fashion.

"What's brought you out here so late in the evening?" Heather asked.

"I was going stir-crazy in my apartment," Liv explained. "I needed to get out. And next thing I knew, I was here. I hope it's okay. I should have called first."

"It's fine," Heather assured her. "We were wrapping up anyway."

Liv bit her lip, uncertainty lighting up her eyes. "I was thinking about what Tyler said this morning about staying together to help each other through our loss." Her voice broke on the word. "I was hoping you'd let me stay here. I don't have to be back to work until Friday afternoon. I just can't be in the apartment anymore."

Sympathetic to Liv's grief, Heather debated the wisdom of inviting her to stay. But short of telling her about the drug ring, Heather couldn't really say no. "I'll make up—" Heather swallowed back the sudden lump of sorrow "—Seth's bed for you."

Relief swept over Liv's face. "Thank you. I'll go get my bag."

Liv left the room and went out the back door.

Tyler scoffed. "She packed a bag."

Heather was perplexed, too. But then again, she'd never really understood Liv. Heather had been looking forward to getting to know her better and to calling her sister. An ache throbbed in Heather's chest. She'd never have a sister now.

Liv returned with a large designer bag in tow. "I was also hoping you'd have some childhood photos of Seth," she said as she dragged her bag all the way inside. "I'd like to get started on a memorial board."

Heather gritted her teeth. She'd thought she'd been clear that morning she wasn't up for tackling a memorial for Seth. "Yes, we have photos. They're stored in the attic. But, Liv, I'm not ready to do this."

"I will take care of it," Liv said as tears welled. She blinked several times, visibly gathering her composure. "I need the closure. Point me in the right direction, and I'll find what we need."

Closure. Heather wouldn't have closure until she knew who'd killed her brother. But she couldn't tell Liv that. "I'll show you where they are." She turned to Tyler. "The key to the carriage apartment is under the doormat. We keep the place stocked, so it should be ready to go."

He held her gaze. "You'll call me if you need anything?"

"Of course," she assured him. He'd programed his number into her cell phone already and had made her promise to keep the phone on her person at all times.

"Where's Colin?" Liv asked.

"In bed," Heather replied. "We had a big day."

Disappointment dampened the other woman's expression. "I didn't get to see him this morning either. I could really use one of his hugs."

Heather had no words for Liv. She wasn't about to tell the woman to go wake Colin.

"I'll check in with you later," Tyler said, throwing his backpack over his shoulder. "Nice to see you again, Liv."

"And you," Liv replied politely.

Once Tyler left the house, the exhaustion that Heather had kept at bay threatened to send her to her knees. But Liv was staring at her expectantly, so Heather bolstered her stamina. She would get through this. She sent up a silent prayer for God's strength. "Follow me."

A few hours later, with the kitchen table covered in Heather's and Seth's childhood photos, Heather accepted a second cup of tea from Liv, who'd taken it upon herself to boil more water and scramble some eggs for them both. Once they'd brought the boxes of pictures down from the attic, Heather had intended to walk away and leave Liv to her project, but for some macabre reason, Heather needed to see the photos, even though the memories created pain deep in her core.

"These photos are wonderful," Liv said as she took her seat next to Heather. "I so wish I could have met your parents. They seem like the best."

"They were." Heather picked up a family photo taken at Christmas Heather's freshman year of high school. Seth was so young and gangly in the photo. Heather had thought herself so trendy in her skinny jeans, cropped cardigan and slipper boots that were comfortable but not functional. Her parents had looked so happy, so alive.

Her heart pulsed with anguish. She missed them so much. They'd been so caring and supportive. Of both her and Seth. She remembered how proud her father was to walk her down the aisle when she married Ken. And she also remembered her father's tears at Ken's military funeral.

Heather hadn't cried until the folded flag had been placed in her hands. Then the numbness had broken. Her mother had held her in her arms. That moment was imprinted on Heather's heart like a scar.

To hide the tears burning behind her eyes from Liv, she sipped from her tea.

"I love this picture of Seth." Liv held up a photo from his high school graduation.

Heather remembered that night. After the ceremony, Seth had taken off. Her parents had been frantic when he hadn't returned. And when he did show up three days later, he was high and combative. Her parents had hidden the incident from her. Like so many other times.

It wasn't until after Ken died that her parents had confessed that Seth was in a bad way. Heather had been grieving her husband but had come home to talk some sense into Seth. He'd tuned her out. She'd gone back to Washington, only returning for holidays and then after the tragic car accident two years ago that had claimed her parents' lives.

Pressure built within Heather. Suddenly nauseated, she quickly rose. "I need some fresh air."

She stumbled out to the porch, down the stairs and hurried around the side of the house where she dry heaved into the barren rosebushes.

Wrapping her arms around her middle, more to keep herself from breaking into a million pieces than from the cold, she walked away from the house to the lone lodge pole tree in the backyard. At the base of the tree was a bench where her father would often sit to whittle.

She sank down on the bench. Snow flurries swirled

in the air, but she hardly noticed or cared. All that had happened over the past week crashed in on her. Everything hurt. The first tear slid slowly down her cheek. The rest came out in gushing sobs. Dropping her face into her hands, she let loose the grief she'd bottled up inside.

The snap of a branch blasted through her sorrow. With dawning horror, she realized how foolish she'd been to leave the safety of the house. She jumped to her feet. In her peripheral vision she saw movement. Panicked, she ran and prayed she made the safety of the house in time.

SEVEN

"Heather!" Tyler called out in a hushed tone as he caught up to her and gripped her elbow to stop her from running away.

Heather froze, her body rigid.

"Tyler!" She whirled to confront him. The shadows concealed her expression, but moonlight glistened on the flakes of snow landing in her dark hair, creating little sparks that matched the anger in her tone. "You scared me."

Contrite, he rubbed his hands up and down her arms. "Sorry. I didn't mean to."

She let out a trembling breath. "What are you doing out here?"

"I was walking the perimeter and I saw you come outside." He wished he could see her face. "Are you ill?"

"No." The stiffness left her body. Her shoulders slumped, and her voice quivered. "Just overwhelmed."

Hurting for her, he led her back to the bench and eased them both down to sit side by side. He shed his jacket and draped it over her shoulders, keeping his arm loosely around her. The frigid night air seeped through his T-shirt. "You shouldn't have come outside alone."

"I know. I wasn't thinking." She sat with her spine

straight as if to avoid leaning too much on him. She tried so hard to be independent. Was that why he felt such an insane desire to ease her load, to take care of her?

Needing a distraction from his thoughts, he changed the subject. "It must have been hard to look at pictures of your past," he said softly. His fingertips drew small circles on her biceps.

"Yes." She sniffled.

He tensed, unsure how to deal with a crying woman. Then something his grandmother said came to mind. "It's okay to cry. My gran always told me crying was the heart's way of letting out the bad stuff to make room for the good stuff."

"She sounds like a smart woman."

"Gran was my rock. She'd held me together so many times as a kid."

"Was?"

Sorrow pinched his heart. "She and Gramps are gone now."

A shudder worked through Heather. He pulled her close. Alarm bells went off in his head, but he ignored them. She needed comfort right now, and he knew she wouldn't ask for it. It was the least he could offer her, considering he'd scared her. Not to mention upset her life even more than it had been by revealing her brother's less than honorable actions. Holding her now had nothing to do with opening up to her earlier, revealing his private pain. He wasn't sure why he'd done that. Maybe because of all the people in his life, she'd be the one to understand. She, too, had been touched by drug addiction. A bond shared was a powerful thing indeed.

For a moment she resisted, and then she melted into his arms. Her silent tears soaked through his T-shirt where her cheek rested against his chest. For a long moment he held her as she cried. Her tears didn't scare him as he'd thought they would. He doubted she'd let very many people see her break down before. For some reason that made his ego puff up for a moment.

But then reality dawned, and he squashed his inflated ego. Comforting her wasn't about him. She was so busy being strong for her son, for Liv, for her employees. That she felt safe enough with him to lower her defenses only told him how much she needed to let loose. Bottling up all the emotion couldn't be good for her or her son.

That was all that mattered.

She shivered and burrowed in closer. "It's snowing."

The flakes were bigger now and sticking to the ground.

"Come on—let's get you inside," he said as he pulled her to her feet. After he tucked her in close to his body, they walked across the lawn, leaving a trail of footsteps in their wake. Side by side they climbed the stairs to the back porch. She hesitated at the door. He gave her a questioning look.

"Thank you," she said softly, laying both of her hands on his chest, covering the stain of her tears. The warmth of her touch sank through him, heating his heart, making it feel full. Complete…

"You're welcome." Gazing into her lovely eyes, so pretty with specks of gold and green. They made him think of picnics and warm, lazy days. His gaze dropped to her mouth. Full lips, red from the cold. Such a pretty mouth. So kissable.

She glanced up and then made a small noise of dismay before stepping back. He followed her gaze to the sprig of mistletoe hanging from the eave above him.

Without another word, she opened the door and stepped inside, leaving the door open for him. Disappointment engulfed him. He scrubbed a hand over his whiskered jaw and called himself a jerk for thinking about kissing her when she'd been so upset. But the reality was he wanted to kiss the lovely Heather, and he'd be kidding himself if he denied that fact. And if she hadn't retreated when she had, he might have weakened and given in to the temptation to kiss her.

He filled his lungs with the fresh, freezing air to cool down his blood and calm his racing heart.

Why was it every time he was around Heather, he lost focus on the job?

His fascination with her had to stop.

Now.

Though he knew he should return to the carriage house over the detached garage and create some distance between himself and Heather, he didn't feel right deserting her when she was so upset. That was all. So instead of beating a hasty retreat he entered the farmhouse and shut the door behind him. Warmth from the central heating chased away the chill from outside. Heather stood at the kitchen counter sipping from a mug, her gaze everywhere but on him. Liv sat at the dining table, surrounded by photographs.

Liv glanced inquisitively from him to Heather and back.

But she didn't comment.

"I'm going to check on Colin," Heather said before hurrying from the room.

Rising from her seat at the table, Liv speared him with a hard look that was so different from the mushy mess she'd been earlier. "What are your intentions toward Heather?"

Taken aback by both the question and that Liv was taking it on herself to be Heather's champion, he sought for a neutral tone as he answered. "We're friends. Business partners. Nothing more."

She pointed one red-tipped nail at him. "Don't play with her affections. She's been through enough trauma in her life."

Half offended and half pleased by her concern for Heather, he said, "I wouldn't dream of hurting Heather. Or Colin."

"You better not," Liv stated in a firm tone that didn't quite match his perception of her. "I'll be watching you."

He suppressed a chuckle. "It's good to know you're watching out for her best interest."

Liv nodded. "I am. I was going to be her sister, you know." She moved back to the table. "Just because Seth is gone doesn't mean I should stop caring about Heather and Colin."

"Of course not." Tyler stepped to the table and stared at the images spread out before him. Heather had been a cute kid and a pretty teen. The happy pictures of her family seared him clean through. She deserved to be happy again. She and Colin deserved so much more than a man like him. Not that he was asking to be their man. But seeing these images brought home how very different their lives had been and how different their futures were.

And how a relationship with Heather was an impossible dream. A dream he needed to put out of his mind.

When Heather returned a few moments later to report Colin was still fast asleep, Tyler took his leave.

"Good night, ladies." He shut the door behind him and made his way back to the carriage house. He paused at the top of the stairs leading to the apartment door. His gaze swept across the view of the house, the work buildings and rows and rows of trees. All was peaceful, quiet. But for how long?

At some point the people responsible for Seth's death would surface with their drugs. And when that time came, he and the team would be ready. He could only hope it happened before all his defenses crumbled and he allowed the sweet and tempting Heather to breech the barricades of his heart. He could still feel the heat of her touch. He put his hand over his heart as if doing so would be enough to block Heather from getting inside.

The next morning, Heather had her emotions back under control. She was so embarrassed about her sobfest last night. Thankfully, poor Tyler had endured her tears, and for that she was grateful. But he wasn't here to be her shoulder to cry on. He was here to bring down a drug ring and find her brother's killer.

That was reason enough to keep a firm rein on her control and not give in to the need to lean on Tyler, to long for his kisses. And, oh, boy, did she. When they'd been standing there at her back door, the tenderness in his eyes had melted her heart into a puddle, and for a moment she'd been on the verge of rising on tiptoe to close the gap between them. But then she'd spied the green mistletoe with the red ribbon hanging overhead and reality slapped her upside the head.

Kissing him wasn't something she could allow. Not now, not ever. She had to think of Colin. She had to maintain control of her emotions to be everything her son needed despite how good it had felt to release her anguish. She'd kept all her suffering locked up inside, thinking it would make her strong. Letting it out had had the desired effect. She was infused with renewed strength, energy.

Tyler's words floated through her mind, and she smiled. She liked the idea of relinquishing the bad to make room for the good. She could use some good right about now.

But freeing her inner torment hadn't quelled her queasy stomach. This morning was not much better. She prayed she wasn't getting sick. The last thing she needed was to be laid up with the flu.

After dressing, she checked Colin's room, but he wasn't there. A bubble of concern stirred her nausea. Clamping her lips together, she hurried downstairs to find Colin and Liv sitting on the couch watching a kid's show with the volume low. Relief swept through her like a clean wave, but it did nothing to quell her upset stomach.

"Mommy!" Colin cried when he noticed her. He jumped up and raced into her waiting arms.

She swung him up and kissed him noisily, loving his laughter.

Liv walked past them into the kitchen. "I'll make French toast. Anybody want some?"

"Me!" Colin pushed at Heather's arms. She released him, and he ran into the kitchen.

Following at a more sedate pace, Heather noticed the dining table had been cleared except for a stack of photos and a large three-sided display board.

A knock at the back door drew her attention. She pushed the curtain aside and wasn't surprised to see Tyler. Sunlight bathed him in a soft glow. He'd shaved and changed into jeans and a plaid button-down shirt beneath Seth's old shearling jacket. Her heart did a little jig in her chest. Remembering what a mess she'd been last night raised her blood pressure.

Stifling the urge to do an about-face and head out

the front door, she opened the back door instead and stepped aside so he could enter. "Good morning."

Though he smiled, there was a determination in his eyes that hadn't been there yesterday. "Morning."

"Mr. Tyler!" Colin ran straight at him.

Tyler lifted him high and then set him on his feet. "Little man, how are you today?"

"Good. Aunt Liv is making French toast."

The shock of hearing her son call Liv *Aunt* reverberated through Heather and dislodged a shard of grief to pierce her heart. She supposed there was no harm in Colin referring to Liv with the familial title. If Seth had lived, Liv would have been Colin's aunt.

"Would you like to join us?" Liv called out from the kitchen. "There's plenty."

At his questioning glance, Heather nodded her encouragement.

"Sure, I'd love that," he said to Liv, but his attention remained on Heather.

Suddenly hot, she tugged at the collar of her sweater.

"It's beautiful outside." He shed the jacket and hung it on the back of a chair. "The layer of snow makes everything look so pristine."

"Hopefully it won't melt." Like she was doing beneath his heated gaze.

Heather escaped into the kitchen to gather plates and utensils. She set the table, skirting around Tyler but pausing slightly to inhale his aftershave. A woodsy scent that brought to mind cozy nights curled up on the couch by the hearth. Her mouth went dry.

"Sit down," Liv ordered. "Breakfast is served." She carried in a plate piled with thick slices of egg-dipped bread that had been cooked to golden brown on both sides.

Heather hadn't expected to have much of an appetite, but she easily ate two pieces. Liv kept up a running dialogue of stories about her clientele at the beauty salon she owned. When they were done, Tyler helped Heather clear the table.

"Liv, we've got this," he said when Liv followed them into the kitchen.

Apparently he wanted to talk to Heather alone. She hoped he didn't bring up last night. She owed him an apology. However, she had no desire to talk about her mini-breakdown.

A frown puckered Liv's perfectly plucked eyebrows. "Are you sure?"

"Yes," Tyler said. To Heather he said, "I'll wash—you dry."

Heather opened a drawer and took out a clean dish towel. "Sounds good."

Liv shrugged and left the room.

As soon as the other woman was out of earshot, Heather said, "Sorry about last night."

He scrubbed a dish. "No worries." He handed her the plate. "I've been thinking." He lowered his voice. "What if Seth stashed the notebook in the Christmas Village?"

Placing the dried plate in the cupboard, she contemplated Tyler's question. "He might have. Though there would be a greater possibility of discovery by just about anyone."

"Not if he disguised the journal," Tyler countered. "I remember peering into a couple of storefronts that had bookshelves."

Why hadn't she thought of that? "I think you're onto something there. I remember once he hid a book that my parents disapproved of in the tailor shop."

"There you go."

"I did promise Colin we could help Rob some more today."

"That would be the perfect cover for looking around," Tyler said in an accent that made her think of Inspector Clouseau from the Pink Panther movies.

She smiled but didn't dare try an accent. "Yes, it would."

He waggled his eyebrows. "Then it's a plan."

She laughed, liking his playful side. They finished cleaning up the breakfast dishes, and then she got Colin ready to go outside.

Knowing the polite thing to do was invite Liv, Heather asked, "Would you care to join us?"

Liv waved her hand and sat at the dining table again. "I'm going to work on the memorial board." She picked up the stack of photos and laid them out on the table.

Afraid she'd tear up again, Heather turned away from the pictures. With Colin between them, she and Tyler walked across the property, through the trees and past the cabins to the Christmas Village.

Most of the decorations had been finished the day before. A few employees swept the wooden walkways. Others had put down sand to smooth out the graveled ground. Today the petting zoo was being assembled. At the back of the large pen where the animals would roam free was a large-scale nativity scene with mannequin Joseph, Mary and baby Jesus in a manger. A large star hung over the baby from a pole that had been attached to the back of the pen.

"You go all out here," Tyler commented.

"We do," she agreed.

Rob was standing with a man Heather didn't recognize near the Toy Shoppe. The outside of the shop had been painted red with white trim. Two large windows flanked the door. In one window an array of china dolls stared out at them with unblinking eyes. The other window had various-sized stuffed teddy bears and an assorted display of old-fashioned toys made from wood, some of which her father had crafted.

As Heather, Tyler and Colin approached, Rob broke off his conversation with the young man, saying, "We'll discuss this more later."

The young man nodded and sauntered away.

Colin tugged his hand loose from Heather's to run to Rob. The older man ruffled his hair.

Exchanging a curious glance with Tyler, Heather asked Rob, "What was that about?" Her gaze strayed to the man heading out of the village.

"That is Paul Ambrose," Rob said. "Dean Ambrose's kid."

Though she recognized the name, she couldn't put a face to it.

"Dean usually drives the sleigh," Rob supplied. "But he's having some health issues, and Paul has volunteered to take his father's place."

"That's kind of him," Heather said. "Does he know how to drive the sleigh?"

Rob shrugged. "Better than I do." He shifted on his cane. "We're almost ready here."

"Yesterday I didn't get a chance to show Tyler the different buildings." She gestured to the toy shop. "Is it unlocked?"

"It's not." Rob held out a ring of keys. "The red key opens that door."

"Who, besides you, has keys to the buildings?" Tyler asked.

"Seth had a set." Rob frowned. "Not sure where they ended up."

"I didn't see them in his room," Heather said. "Could they be in the barn?"

Rob shook his head. "I didn't see them in the tack room or any of the stalls."

She unlocked the door and pushed it open. Inside the air was musty and stale. A layer of dust coated everything.

"Look, Mommy, my old tricycle!" Colin sat on the blue trike, his long legs scrunched up to his chin, and rode forward a few inches.

"Hey, buddy, why don't we take that outside," Tyler said.

Colin jumped up to drag the trike to the door. Tyler helped him get it outside.

Grateful to Tyler for his care of her son, Heather stepped past a rocking horse to the workbench made to look as if the toy maker were in the process of building a dollhouse. The dust here had been disturbed as if someone had laid something across the bench. Behind the half-made dollhouse she found a leather-bound book.

Excitement accelerated her breathing. Could this be Seth's mysterious journal? She opened the book to find it was a ledger with the farm's payables and receivables for the past two years.

The corner of a white envelope sticking out from inside a small cubbyhole in the workbench caught her attention. She tugged the envelope out and found more than a dozen similar envelopes. Curious, she opened one and found an overdue bill dated last month. Her heart beat a frantic tune as she opened each envelope. They were all overdue bills. Some so past overdue that a collection agency had sent notices.

Her stomach sank. She began to understand. So this was why Seth had gone into business with a drug cartel. But why hadn't he told her the farm wasn't making a profit? And how long had this been going on?

Tucking the envelopes into her coat pocket and clutching the ledger under her arm, she went outside to find Tyler. He leaned against the railing, encouraging Colin as he rode the tricycle up and down the walkways, his little legs pumping as fast as he could. The tenderness on Tyler's face stopped her breath.

The man might claim to not have any experience with children, but he obviously had a soft spot for them. Or at least for Colin. An ache of longing hit her so hard she fell back a step from the blow.

She wanted Colin to have a father. She wanted a husband to call her own. She wanted what she'd lost when Ken died.

Guilt for even contemplating replacing Ken in her heart, in her son's heart, charged through her, setting her nerves on a sharp edge. She fought the urge to steady herself with a hand on the building's outside wall. She had to get a firm handle on her feelings. Right now.

Tyler looked her way. She prayed he didn't notice she was upset. Squaring her shoulders and lifting her chin, she repaired the crumbling shield around her heart as best she could. She had too many other things to worry about right now. She didn't want to have to deal with her uncooperative heart craving something she couldn't allow herself to have.

"What's that?" Tyler said, his gaze on the book in her hands.

His eager tone propelled her to his side. "It's the farm's accounting records."

"Oh." There was no mistaking the disappointment in the word.

"I need to go into town and reconcile the farm's finances." She pulled the envelopes of unpaid bills from her jacket pocket. "Seth wasn't paying the bills. I have no idea where the farm stands financially."

"Does your family have a safe-deposit box where Seth might have hidden the journal?"

"I don't know. My parents never mentioned one."

"Any chance your brother might have opened one?"

She shrugged. "If he did, he never told me about it. But, then again, there seems to be a great deal he never shared with me."

It hurt to realize how little she actually knew of Seth's life and the secrets he kept. Secrets that put them all in jeopardy.

And had put her on a collision course with a wonderful man who had her emotions spinning out of control and made her long for things that could never be.

EIGHT

"I can't believe Seth did this." Heather clutched the leather-bound ledger with the farm's bank records inside to her as Tyler started up the engine of his truck. She sat in the passenger seat and stared out the window at the passing scenery. Her stomach hurt; so did her heart.

She and Tyler had just come from the bank in Bonners Ferry where they'd gone over the farm's financials with the bank manager and were now on their way back home. She'd left Colin with Liv. Blake and Nathanial had promised to keep an eye on the house, so Heather wouldn't worry.

But *worry* was such a mild word for how she felt now that she'd learned Seth had put the farm in a precarious financial situation. He'd siphoned a good portion of the farm's income to purchase personal big-ticket items. The new car that Olivia drove, the down payment on the town house he had intended to share with Liv once they married and the beautiful diamond engagement ring that Liv wore. Not to mention the deposit on a honeymoon package to the Cayman Islands.

"It seems your brother had made more than a few bad decisions," Tyler commented, taking the turn off the highway onto the road leading to the tree farm.

"Understatement of the millennium. Bad decisions and lying to me. When I asked Seth about Liv's ring, he claimed he'd been saving up. I had no idea he had paid for her car or the town house. I wrongly assumed those were Liv's expenses." Her fingers tightened around the ledger. "If we don't turn a profit this season, I don't know what will happen to the farm. To Colin and me."

The thought of losing her family home was like a physical blow. The nausea she'd been trying to ignore for the past several hours intensified. She swallowed several times to keep bile from burning her throat.

Up ahead the Christmas Village came into view. So festive and inviting. It was late enough in the day that most of the employees who didn't live on the farm had left for the day and wouldn't return until Friday morning when the farm opened to the public.

Tomorrow was Thanksgiving.

She let out a groan.

Tyler shot her a glance. "What's up?"

"I didn't get a turkey. Or anything else, for that matter. And Thanksgiving is tomorrow. I always fix a meal for the staff who stay behind." She sighed. "My grandmother and mom both did. Now I've dropped the ball."

He reached over and took her hand. "I'll take care of it."

His big warm hand engulfed hers, offering comfort and protection. She wanted to lean on this man. To let him shoulder some of her burdens, her concerns. It had been so long since she'd had someone to share her load with that the weight of her troubles threatened to bury her. But it would be selfish of her to slough off her duties and obligations. Wouldn't it?

Not to mention dangerous. She couldn't let herself

become too dependent on him; doing so would only lead to more heartache when he left.

"I can't ask you to do that," she said, withdrawing her hand from his. "I'll have the grocery store deliver what we'll need for tomorrow's feast." It would cost twice as much, but what choice did she have?

"Seriously, let the guys and me take care of everything." He brought the truck to a halt at the back steps of the farmhouse. "You've enough to contend with right now."

"You're sweet to want to help," she said. "But I don't think catering a meal for my employees is in your job description."

"But it is." He cut the engine and swiveled to face her. "This will give us a good opportunity to interact with the employees. And while they are all gathered eating, Blake and Nathanial can search the farm without prying eyes."

He made a good case. But… "Letting you take over doesn't sit well."

"Why not?"

"I don't like the fact that I'm losing control of my life." And her heart if she wasn't careful. Two good reasons to say no to his proposal.

"You can supervise," he said with a smile that had her heart fluttering.

Maybe that would work. And truthfully, the thought of putting together a Thanksgiving dinner completely overwhelmed her given what had gone on in the past few days. She was spent. Besides, as he'd said, it would be good for the investigation, and the sooner the investigation was over, the sooner her life would go back to normal. Whatever normal was anymore.

As much as it galled her to hand this over to him,

doing so would be for the best all around. "That would be fine. Thank you." She dropped her gaze to the ledger in her lap. "What am I going to say to Liv? Seth spent money that wasn't his to spend. Liv will have to give up the town house and the car at the very least."

"You'll find the right words when the time is right." Tyler lifted her chin with a finger, forcing her to meet his gaze. "You are not alone in this, Heather. I'm here to help you. But more importantly, God is with you."

How did Tyler do that? He understood what she was feeling when she hadn't even admitted to herself how alone and lonely she felt. A chunk of her heart melted.

But Tyler was temporary. When this was over, he'd leave. And she and Colin would have to learn to live without him or anyone else. It would be just the two of them against the world.

She didn't want to think about that yet. Didn't have the mental fortitude just now. For the time being she was grateful to have Tyler's stable and calm company. Tyler and his team, that was.

They left the truck and entered the house. Colin and Liv were seated at the dining table playing Candy Land. Seeing them together brought a pang of sorrow. Liv doted on Colin and would have made a wonderful aunt.

"Mommy, I'm winning," Colin boasted with a big grin.

A rush of love infused Heather, taming the worries about the farm's financial situation. As long as her son was safe and healthy, nothing else really mattered. Tyler was right—God would protect them and provide for them. She couldn't let circumstance diminish her faith.

Her faith was stronger than that. She only hoped she was stronger than her attraction to Tyler.

* * *

Nathanial rubbed his hands together. "A real American Thanksgiving dinner."

The Canadian's enthusiasm brought a smile to Tyler's lips. He sat on a rickety chair inside the cabin in which the two IBETs members were staying in.

Two extra-long twin beds took up half the space, while a small table, chairs and kitchenette took up the rest. A community restroom with showers was a few paces outside the door.

Heather was right when she'd said the cabin would barely be big enough for the two men. Since Liv was there with Heather and Colin, Tyler had risked taking fifteen minutes to update the guys on the situation and asking for their help in providing a Thanksgiving feast for the dozen or so people who would remain on the tree farm tomorrow. "You up for the challenge?"

"Better believe it." Nathanial's lit-up expression reminded Tyler of a kid in a candy store. "Would we be having the marshmallow yam dish? I had that once years ago." He smacked his lips. "Yum, yum."

"You mean sweet potato pie," Blake drawled, letting his Southern twang out in all its glory. "I will make my mama's recipe. There's nothing better."

"As long as there's turkey and gravy, I'm sure everyone will be happy." Tyler opened his wallet and thumbed out several large bills. "This should cover the expense."

Blake took the money, then eyed him with concern. "You're getting invested in this woman and her problems."

He clearly wasn't referring to the case in his hands. Tyler wouldn't deny the statement. Instead he deflected the comment. "I'm invested in seeing this assignment through. If that means paying for a fancy meal cooked by you two, then so be it."

"Be careful, bro," Blake said with a dose of censure in his tone. "Someone's gonna get hurt. They always do."

Tyler studied the other man. "You speaking from experience?"

Blake's jaw hardened. "This isn't about me. That kid's growing attached to you. Not to mention the mom."

Guilt scratched at Tyler's conscience. "I'm not making promises I can't keep. I've been straight with Heather. She understands the priority is bringing down the drug ring."

"And finding her brother's killer," Blake stated.

"Yes, that, too." Though Tyler was positive they were one and the same.

"To that end," Nathanial interjected, "the trucks are scheduled to leave tomorrow, late afternoon. If we're going to find out how the drugs are being smuggled out, we have a very short window of time."

"True." Tyler rose. "So here's the plan. One of you goes into town and does the shopping. While you're there, look into Liv's town house. Find out who holds the loan. Heather's going to need that down payment back."

Blake wagged his head. "Man, what are you doing? That isn't our business."

"Technically, no, it's not, but—"

"But nothing," Blake cut him off.

Nathanial held up a hand. "Time out. I'll head to town." He pointed at Blake. "You make a shopping list." Nathanial opened the cabin door. "Tyler, you get back to the lady and her son. You were tasked with their protection. We'll do our part."

Thankful for Nathanial's level head, Tyler rose. "I appreciate it."

He left the cabin, but Blake's words hounded him all the way back to the farmhouse. After checking in on Heather and Colin, seeing that they were safe, Tyler headed to the carriage house to ponder how he'd let himself get so involved in Heather's well-being, not just physically keeping her safe, but her emotional well-being. He really needed to put the kibosh on the latter because it was wreaking havoc with *his* emotional well-being.

Blake was right. Any way Tyler played it, someone was going to get hurt. Letting himself care too much would jeopardize his judgment, not to mention set him up for disappointment. Or worse, he would end up disappointing Heather and her son.

He needed to distance himself from the mother and child. Though he couldn't physically distance himself, he could be more detached, more professional.

That meant no more hanging around her for the sake of being near her, no more touching her and definitely no more thoughts of kissing her.

Unfortunately, he had a feeling detachment would be a harder battle to win than bringing down a drug cartel.

While Nathanial stayed at the farmhouse with the ladies talking turkey and desserts, Tyler and Blake took advantage of the cover of night to inspect the refrigerated trucks. Tyler knew the Canadian would protect Heather, Liv and Colin. He was a good guy, trustworthy. Yet Tyler couldn't ignore the bits of jealousy that clung to him as he and Blake made their way to the loaded trucks by the light of the moon.

"You take that one," Blake said, pointing to the first truck. "I'll take the other one."

Tyler acknowledged Blake with a thumbs-up, though he wasn't sure the other agent could see him. Starting with the cab, Tyler inspected the inside compartment, checking the obvious places first like the glove box, under the seats, in the door panels and in the sleeping bunk behind the captain's chairs. He pried off the door panels, felt around the headliner and checked under the mats for secret cubbyholes. Nothing.

Using his penlight, he checked the engine, the body panels, the chassis and differential for signs of tampering. No scratch marks, no uneven alignment.

Frustrated by the lack of evidence, he figured the concealed drugs must be inside the refrigerated truck with the Christmas trees. He opened the back doors. A foul odor emanated from inside the box. He faced a mound of trees wrapped in thin netting to condense the size of the trees while protecting them from damage during transport. There had to be at least a hundred trees filling the whole box.

Great. He'd have to unload all the trees to search inside for a hidden compartment.

He grasped the end of the closest tree and tugged. The whole stack shifted. Concerned the whole lot would come shooting out, he let go. His hand came away with a sticky residue that smelled so bad his eyes watered. "What in the world?"

He shone his penlight on the tree and inspected the stem. A thin cut circled the trunk about a half inch from the butt end.

"Find anything?" Blake asked as he approached.

"Something odd." Tyler showed Blake the tree trunk.

"That is odd. And smelly." Blake leaned closer. "Hmm, deer urine."

Tyler cringed. "Yuck. Did you come across something worth mentioning?"

"Nope. That truck hasn't been filled with trees yet. I couldn't find any hidey-holes for drugs inside or outside."

Disappointed, Tyler shut the box door. "I want Heather to take a look at this tree. And I need to wash my hand."

"I second that."

When they reached the farmhouse, pie prep was in full swing. Tyler stopped in the doorway. "Heather, can I see you for a moment?"

They stepped out onto the back porch.

Heather's nose wrinkled. "What have you been doing?"

"Apparently a deer used a tree before it was cut down." He hid his hand behind his back, but that did nothing to alleviate the smell.

"Ugh. We do have a whitetail deer herd that comes through when the weather turns cold. You really should go scrub your hand. Deer carry some nasty diseases."

"I don't want to smell up your house," he said.

"I'll be right back." Heather hurried inside. A few minutes later she returned with a wet, soapy washcloth, a dry towel and a dish of water.

Taking the washcloth, he wiped his hand, then rinsed in the water she held. Using the towel, he said, "Thank you. That's much better."

"If I were you, I'd do another scrub at the sink."

"I will, thanks."

She set the bowl aside on the wooden porch. "What did you find?"

"Nothing. Or maybe something. I need you to look at a tree in one of the trucks."

"Let me grab my coat." She gathered the soiled cloths and bowl, then headed back inside. When she returned, she'd put on her red parka. She handed him a pair of work gloves. "So you don't get smelly again."

Her thoughtfulness touched him. The moon's glow illuminated the night enough for them to walk side by side to the box truck. He pulled on the gloves and opened the door.

"Whew!" Heather pinched her nose. "Wow, I never realized how stinky the trees could be."

With his gloved hand, he grasped the tree with the cut. Shining his penlight on the trunk, he asked, "Is this normal?"

"No. That's odd. Does the cut go all the way through?"

"Good question." He tugged, and it loosened. Slowly, he pulled and twisted until the very end of the trunk popped off like a cork. "Well, what do we have here?"

Stuffed inside the hollowed-out trunk was a package wrapped up airtight in plastic and duct tape.

"Is that cocaine?"

"I'd say yes." He stuffed the package back inside and jammed the butt back on.

"Hey, what are you doing?" Heather asked. "I thought you wanted to find the drugs so you could bust the ring. Aren't you going to confiscate it?"

He pushed the tree back into place. "Not yet. We don't know who put it there or when or if that's the only tree. The other truck has yet to be loaded. We'll need to catch them in the act."

Heather sighed. "When will this be over?"

Giving in to his need to reassure her, he put his arm around her shoulders and hustled her back to the house. "Not long now. Do you know where that truck is headed?"

"Not offhand, but I'm sure Don will have the itinerary."

"Can you get a hold of him and ask?"

"Sure. Though what reason do I give him for asking? I've never been involved in that part of the farm."

"Just say you're curious. Or better yet, your new business partner is curious."

"Right. My business partner." He heard a smile in her voice. "I can do that."

They went inside where it was warm and smelled like cinnamon and vanilla.

Heather slipped upstairs to make her call. Tyler joined Colin in the living room to watch a holiday cartoon. Taking a seat on the couch, he looked at the television and said, "Hey, I remember this from when I was a kid."

Colin got up from the floor where he'd been lying on his belly and climbed onto the couch right next to Tyler. "It's my favorite."

Affection flooded Tyler as the boy snuggled against his side. Colin was so trusting and innocent. Blake's words came screaming back to Tyler.

Someone's gonna get hurt. They always do.

That kid's growing attached to you.

The last thing he wanted to do was harm this boy in any way. But for the life of him, Tyler couldn't push the child away, nor did he want to move away from him. Sitting like this was so foreign yet so comfortable and natural.

Heather returned a few moments later and stopped in the archway to the living room. Tyler locked gazes with her. The tenderness in her eyes and the small smile on her lips had his heart thumping in his chest. It wasn't good to get her hopes up, either.

He wasn't father material. He didn't know how to relate to children, and he didn't know how to parent. He had no role model to fall back on. Though he'd had his grandparents, they had overcompensated for their daughter's failings by being lenient with him, making his time with them seem more like a vacation than an actual home.

Regretfully, he extracted himself from Colin. Heather gestured to the front door. They stepped outside.

Brimming with excitement, she said, "The one already loaded is headed for Calgary. The other is headed east."

"Okay, now we're getting somewhere." Anticipation revved through his veins. "Who's driving the trucks?"

"Don said he was going to assign drivers to the trucks tomorrow. He said he has three volunteers to drive the one across the border. And another three volunteers to drive the other truck."

Tyler stroked his jaw, contemplating the implications. "Six drivers willing to transport the trees. Question is do they know the drugs are inside the trees? I want those six names."

"The thing is we give bonuses to the drivers on Thanksgiving and Christmas Eve. So they may be eager for the bonus rather than having anything to do with the drugs."

That poked a little hole in his hope that one of the six would be the guilty party he sought. Still, they were closer to their objective than they had been. At least now they could confirm that Seth had been telling the truth. They'd found the drugs in the tree. How many more trees held packages of cocaine?

If they could only find the journal, then they could end this for all their sakes.

"Do we have info on the company taking possession of the trees in Canada?"

She handed him a piece of paper. "Don gave me names and contact info."

"Good. I'll pass this on to my boss."

Before he could step down the front stairs, Heather placed her hand on his arm. "Thank you, Tyler."

"I'm doing my job, Heather. Nothing more." He deliberately infused an impersonal tone into his voice.

Hurt bloomed in her eyes, and the look instantly tore at him. He wanted nothing more than to take her in his arms and soothe her worries away. But that would be a mistake.

He wasn't there to play house, and she needed to understand that reality. So did he. He was there on a mission, and he would leave when the mission was accomplished. Tyler couldn't let his feelings for the pretty widow derail this operation by letting things become personal.

He couldn't lose his focus. If he let down his guard, he might miss something that could blow this case wide-open. He had to stop letting Heather and Colin be a distraction to his end goal.

With a quick nod, he hurried to the carriage house for privacy to call his boss, who was excited by the new development. "You've done well, Agent Griffin. Now we need to catch these smugglers in the act."

"We'll sit on the trucks tonight," Tyler assured him. "When the second truck is loaded in the morning, we'll round up the employees. They won't have any choice but to cooperate. Then Blake and I will drive the drugs north. I'd like to leave Nathanial here as protection for the Larson-Randall family."

"Sounds like a plan," Granger said. "I'll coordinate with the Royal Canadian Mounted Police and be ready to move in once the trees are delivered."

"Great. Thank you, sir," Tyler said before hanging up.

When he returned to the farmhouse, he drew Heather into the hall and whispered, "Can you have Liv take Colin upstairs without raising any questions?"

Concern darkened her eyes. "Yes, what's up?"

"I need to talk to you and the guys, privately."

Though he could see she wanted more information, she pressed her lips together and strode back into the kitchen where Liv, Nathanial and Blake were busy cooking. The place was a disaster zone.

"Liv, would you be willing to take Colin up and get him ready for bed?" Heather asked.

"Of course." Liv dropped the dough she was kneading onto the wooden cutting board, whipped off her apron and washed her hands before hurrying from the room.

"You didn't have to ask her twice," Nathanial observed.

"She loves Colin," Heather said. Turning to Tyler, she put her hands on her hips. "So tell us. What's the plan?"

He quickly outlined what he and Granger had decided.

Heather frowned. "You're leaving?"

He didn't like the guilt clawing up his neck, but there was no help for it. He had a job to do. "After the feast tomorrow. I promised we'd help you with that."

"Hey, I'll be here," Nathanial said. "Once these lugs leave."

She sent him a polite smile. "That'd be great."

When she swept past Tyler, she shot him a half bewildered, half hurt look that constricted his chest. In her eyes he was letting her down. And that realization hit him harder than the knowledge that he'd let things get too personal between them and that it had to stop.

NINE

Heather paced her darkened bedroom Thanksgiving eve. The house was quiet. Colin slept soundly in his bed, and Liv was asleep in Seth's room. Heather had been surprised by how well Liv was holding up. After her initial tears, Liv had been energetic in helping the guys prepare for the Thanksgiving feast. She'd bathed Colin and put him to bed after reading him several stories.

Heather was thankful Colin liked Liv, but she couldn't help worry that one day Liv would move on with her life and leave them behind. It seemed everyone left her behind. Ken, her parents, Seth. Now Tyler.

He, too, was leaving. It would be too much to hope that he'd be the one to return her truck. Most likely he'd stay to wrap up his investigation by arresting whoever took possession of the drugs.

She'd known he would eventually leave, but she'd thought, hoped, he'd stay long enough to see that she and Colin were safe and the drug smugglers were no longer a threat. He'd promised he would. Apparently, his promise wasn't something she could count on.

And it wasn't that she didn't trust the other man, Nathanial. She did. It was just that... She couldn't put to words the reason why Tyler leaving so soon felt like he was abandoning her. Them.

She let out a frustrated breath, irritated at herself for being so foolish. He was only doing his job. His promise was to protect her, and if leaving was his way of doing that, then she needed to buck up and deal with his absence. Yes, Tyler leaving was for the best; she'd begun to rely on him too much, to look forward to seeing him and wanting to share her thoughts with him. Things she'd missed since Ken's death.

Pushing back the curtain, Heather peered out at the farm. Another layer of snow had fallen to make the world outside bright with the moon's light reflecting off the white powder. She couldn't see Tyler or the others. The guys had left the house an hour ago. Heather had heard them talking about staking out the trucks in the hope that whoever had put the drugs in the harvested trees would come out to check on their stash. If they caught someone, then what?

Would that be the end of it?

She prayed so.

Her breath fogged the window. It was cold out there.

She left her room and silently made her way downstairs to the kitchen. She didn't dare let her mind question what she was doing as she made three thermoses of hot cocoa. With the thermoses in hand, she hesitated. How did she get them to the guys? She couldn't very well go marching across the farm calling out their names.

She figured Tyler would be positioned in a spot where he could watch the truck and the house. Or at least one of the men would be. She hoped.

After putting on her parka, she slipped out the front

door, carrying the hot thermoses. She stood in the shadows, unwilling to venture farther into the moonlight. For a long moment she waited. Then, feeling silly, she shook her head at her own ridiculousness. Even if Tyler could see her, he wouldn't break cover to retrieve hot chocolate.

She reached for the doorknob, intending to go back inside where it was warm and no one could see her embarrassment.

"Heather?" Tyler's whisper floated in the air.

She froze for a long moment, and then slowly turned to find Tyler standing at the bottom of the stairs. She recognized the set of his shoulders and the way he stood with his legs braced slightly apart. Her heart thumped. She was glad he couldn't see her face because she was sure her cheeks were bright red.

"I made you hot chocolate." She held up the thermoses. "And some for the guys."

He vaulted up the stairs to stand beside her. Though it was too dark to see his expression, she could feel his energy swirling around her, stirring up her senses.

"That was sweet of you," he whispered. "You really should go back inside."

"I wanted to apologize."

"For?" He'd moved so close his breath tickled her ear.

Her mouth went suddenly dry. She forced her words past her parched throat. "For not being gracious earlier. You're doing your job, which is to stop the drug ring. Of course you should go with the trees and drugs to Canada."

After taking the thermoses from her, he set them down on the porch, then took her hand and led her to the stairs. They sat on the top one.

Nathanial's voice came through clearly. "Tyler, heads up. The unidentified subject has veered away from the trucks and is making his way toward the house."

The news sent a burst of alarm into Tyler's midsection. "Copy that."

He ducked behind the nearest bushy tree since there was no way he'd make it back to his position in time to stop the guy's advance. Tyler waited, calming his breath and slowing his heart rate, preparing to take the guy down before he got anywhere close to the house.

All was quiet. No nocturnal noises from beast or fowl. *Wait.* The faint rustling of feet slogging through the newly fallen snow reached Tyler. He estimated the intruder was ten feet to his right.

Staying low in case the guy had his own set of night vision goggles, Tyler moved around the backside of the tree, the pine needles tickling his nose. He saw a figure pass by. Sure enough the man had on a pair of night goggles, and he carried a gun in his hand.

Fearing for Heather, Colin and Liv's safety, Tyler knew he couldn't let the man reach the house. As soon as the man broke the tree line and started across the wide expanse of lawn, Tyler rushed at him, driving his shoulder into the man's back, wrapping his arms around the intruder and letting momentum carry them both down to the snowy ground.

"Tyler!" Blake's voice blasted in Tyler's ear. "On my way."

"I can handle this," Tyler huffed out as he and the intruder scuffled for control of the gun, rolling across the wet, cold ground, trading punches and exerting energy in an effort to subdue each other. Moonlight glinted on the ring the guy wore on his middle finger seconds before he landed a hard right cross. Tyler absorbed the blow and, with a deep growl, threw an uppercut and a quick jab aimed for the bridge of the man's nose. He heard the crunch of cartilage breaking, giving Tyler the momentary advantage, which he capitalized on by knocking the gun from the man's hand. It went sliding away.

Lights flooded the yard.

The intruder let out a roar of pain and twisted away from the bright glow of the house's floodlights. Momentarily blinded, Tyler ripped off his night vision goggles with one hand while the other hand grasped the man's jacket. The man had also taken off his goggles and was working to dislodge Tyler's hold.

The door opened, and Heather ran out, hefting a large shotgun. Her red jacket made her a visible target.

Momentarily distracted by the sight, Tyler lost his grip on the assailant. He wiggled away, jumped to his feet and took off at a dead run for the rows of trees.

"He's making a break for it. Southwest of the house through the trees," Tyler said. "I'm securing the house."

"On it," Nathanial said.

"I'm holding my position watching the truck," Blake declared. "This could have just been a distraction."

Agreeing with his colleagues, Tyler moved with purpose to the house. Heather held the shotgun with the barrel pointed downward. The light from the wall fixtures slashed across her anxious face. "He's getting away."

"Nathanial's on his tail."

Her brow was furrowed with worry. "You're hurt."

Ignoring her statement and the pain from where the guy had sent his fist into Tyler's jaw, Tyler wrapped his hand around the long barrel of the shotgun. "Where on earth did you get this?"

"When I was searching for Seth's notebook, I came across my dad's stash of firearms in a safe at the back of the downstairs closet. I had no idea they were there. I wasn't expecting another attack on the house, but I got it out anyway." She shrugged. "I'm glad I didn't need it. And frankly I'm not sure it's loaded. But it looks intimidating."

"And dangerous." Taking the shotgun from her hands, he ushered her inside. "Though I admire your tenacity and bravery, don't ever do that again. Next time I tell you to stay out of sight, you need to stay out of sight."

Her mouth lifted on one side. "You didn't say stay out of sight. You said stay away from the windows."

"Really? You're going to quibble with me on this?"

She shook her head. "No quibbling here. Come into the laundry room and let me take care of the cut on your chin."

Exasperated yet glad she was safe, he followed her to the small laundry room. She dragged a stool out of the corner. "Sit."

He sat down. "It's not that bad."

With an arched eyebrow, she countered, "You haven't seen it."

Rising, he faced the mirror over the sink. A deep slash cut into the skin on his jawline and extended over his chin. "The guy had a ring on."

"Could you identify the ring or the man?" She dabbed his cut with an alcohol swab.

He gritted his teeth against the sting. "Not the ring. The guy's face seemed vaguely familiar, but I only caught a glimpse of him without his goggles on."

She used butterfly bandages to close the wound. "Familiar, huh? That doesn't bode well."

"No, it doesn't."

"What do you think he was after?" Heather met his gaze.

Her green-tinted eyes were round. She was so close. All he'd have to do was lean toward her a fraction of an inch, and their lips would touch. He held himself still by sheer force of will. "Not sure." His voice cracked.

That hadn't happened since he was a teen. But considering he felt like a love-starved teen with hormones racing through his blood, he shouldn't have been surprised. He strove to keep his tone even. "I can only guess that his intention was to see if you knew where Seth's journal was."

She licked her lips. He tracked the moment with his gaze.

"I hope your team catches him," she said, her voice breathless.

Was she struggling with the same attraction that had him in a stranglehold?

"Oh, my." Liv stood in the doorway.

Tyler jerked his gaze away from Heather at the exact moment that she broke contact, as well. Heat clawed up his throat and settled in his face.

Liv's gaze narrowed. "What happened? I heard noises."

Heather backed away from him. "Tyler stopped a trespasser."

"Are we safe?" Liv's expression showed panic.

Tyler stood. "Yes. Everyone is safe." He turned to Heather. "I'll call the local police and loop them in."

She gave him a faint smile. "Thank you."

He slipped past Liv and headed down the hall, thankful not to have succumbed to the temptation to kiss Heather. The last thing either of them needed was Liv witnessing an error in judgment. Especially after he'd assured Liv his intentions toward Heather were purely platonic.

But whether he liked it or not, his feelings for the widow were far from platonic. And that made everything much more complicated.

And if there was one thing he didn't want, it was complications.

"Are you all right?"

Liv's worried expression had Heather blowing out a shaky breath. "Yes. Kind of. I mean, no."

She was scared, freaked out and way too aware of how close she'd just come to kissing Tyler. He'd saved her life twice and that of her family. She shuddered to think what would have happened had the man with the gun slipped past Tyler and broke into her house.

"It was a good thing Tyler was around," Liv said. "Though what was he doing outside, anyway?"

Heather shrugged. "I guess he couldn't sleep and decided to take a walk."

"Hmm. Well, it worked out for us, didn't it?"

Heather put away the first aid kit. "It did, indeed."

"So he's your business partner?" Liv's smirk grated on Heather's nerves.

"Yes," she affirmed in as neutral a tone as she could muster.

"How long have you two known each other?"

"A while." That was vague enough, wasn't it? The last thing she needed was for Liv to prod too deeply into Tyler's cover. Heather yawned. It started out as a fake, but it turned into a real one. "I'm done in."

A knowing look in Liv's gaze made Heather want to squirm. There was no way Liv could guess Tyler's true purpose on the farm. But she'd witnessed the sizzling attraction between Heather and Tyler when she'd walked into the laundry room, much to Heather's chagrin.

"Good night again," Liv said and strode out of the laundry room.

Once she was alone, Heather sat on the stool for a moment and lifted a prayer of thanks to God for protection and for Tyler and his team.

She heard voices coming from the living room. She hurried down the hall to find Nathanial and Blake had joined Tyler. All three men were dressed in dark clothes. They kept their voices low.

"Guy had an ATV stashed in the trees," Nathanial said. "He was prepared for a quick getaway. I tracked the ATV to the road and then lost him. I'll go back out there in the morning and see if I can distinguish his trail."

"Too bad he got away," Blake said. "I'd like to know what he was doing here and who he's working for."

"Wouldn't we all," Tyler commented, frustration evident in his tone.

"I found his gun," Blake said. "An MP9. Slick. I bagged it and will send it in for printing."

Heather had no idea what type of gun that was, but Tyler looked pleased.

"At least that's a start," Tyler said. "You two head on back to the truck, though I doubt we'll see any more action. I'll stand guard here, just in case."

Heather didn't like the "just in case" scenarios playing through her mind. Just in case the intruder tried to break in again. Just in case he brought buddies with him. Just in case Tyler and his team weren't successful a second time around.

When the two men vacated the house, leaving her

and Tyler in the living room, she felt a strange sense of déjà vu. Had it really been only two nights ago he'd entered her life? It seemed like a lifetime.

Strange how easily she'd let him into the very fabric of her life. And she was afraid she was letting him into her heart, as well.

Time to retreat. Yet she couldn't make her feet move. Truth was she didn't want to leave the living room. She didn't want to leave Tyler's side. For that reason alone, she forced herself to say good-night and hurried upstairs.

She'd escaped his presence. But she was pretty sure she wouldn't escape her growing feelings for him quite so easily.

Tyler sat in the darkened living room, his weapon at the ready on his knee. He hated that he'd allowed himself to be distracted by Heather and let the man with the gun escape. It had been a rookie move.

And a testament to how deeply he'd gotten in over his head with the lovely Heather. He'd let her get under his skin, into his mind and definitely into his heart.

He needed this assignment to end so he could move on to a safe one. Safer for his heart, anyway.

There was no way he could let himself believe he had a future with Heather and her adorable son. He wasn't cut out to be a dad, and he wasn't the settle-in-one-place kind of guy. He didn't know how to do domestic. He knew undercover work. He knew taking down bad guys. But being someone's husband, some kid's father? No way.

Yet he couldn't deny that being with Heather and Colin filled him with cravings for a life he'd never known. Would probably never know. He knew better than to say never, but he couldn't envision any other life than the one he led now where he moved from one assignment to another all over the continent. It worked for him. Even if at times it was lonely.

The hours ticked by as the sun slowly made its rise on the eastern horizon. Just as dawn broke, there was a rattle at the front doorknob. Tyler bolted for the door. He unlocked it, grasped the handle and swung the door open in one swift movement. He caught the would-be intruder unaware. A large-framed man tumbled into Tyler, knocking him back several steps. The stench of alcohol hit Tyler in the face like a brick wall. "Whew!"

The intruder wasn't the man Tyler had grappled with the night before. This man was built like a tank with dark hair and a weather-beaten complexion as if he spent his days in the sun without UV protection. Tyler recognized him as one of the men who worked with the trees.

He pushed at Tyler, squirming to get free and yelled, "Mrs. Randall!"

"Whoa! Dude." Tyler wrenched the guy's beefy arm behind his back, whirled him around and drove him face-first into the couch.

"No, you don't understand." The man's slurred words were muffled by the couch cushion. "Mrs. Randall is in trouble. I need to warn her."

Feet pounded down the stairs. Heather skidded to a halt. She wore the same sweats outfit she'd worn the other day. Her hair was messy from sleep, and surprise and panic warred in her eyes. "Ernesto?"

"What's going on?" Liv's sleepy voice cut through the air. She walked out wearing a pink silky robe over a long matching gown and fuzzy pink slippers.

Tyler yanked Ernesto upright. "What do you need to warn Heather about?"

He wobbled on his feet. His gaze darted around until it latched onto Heather. "There are bad people here. You can't trust anyone."

TEN

Heather's heart jumped into her throat. Morning sunlight flooded through the window and open door along with a chill from the cold air temperature outside. Tyler had Ernesto's hands jerked tight behind his back. She reached out a hand to Ernesto. "What do you mean bad people? Who can't I trust?"

Liv made a derisive noise. "He's drunk or high." She marched closer to stare the man in the eye. "He's just trying to make trouble. Or scare you." She shook a finger at the man. "Why would you do this?"

Ernesto's face paled. He whipped his gaze to Heather. "You must call the police."

"You bet we will." Liv reached inside the pocket of her silk wrap for her phone. Within seconds she had the sheriff's department on the line. "This is Liv Dorsett. I'm at the Larson tree farm. We've captured an intruder. You need to come take this crazy man away."

"I'll take Ernesto outside." Tyler gave Heather a look that she interpreted to mean he'd question Ernesto without an audience. He propelled the other man out the front door.

Heather was torn between wanting to hear what Ernesto had to say and needing to keep Liv from following Tyler and finding out that Tyler was more than he claimed.

As Liv headed for the door, Heather made her decision and snagged Liv's hand. "I'm so glad you're here. This is such a nightmare."

Liv frowned at the closed front door, and something dark crossed her face. Heather chalked it up to the fright and anger about the invasion. She felt the same sense of fear and vulnerability. But not because of Ernesto. He couldn't possibly be a part of the drug ring. She'd known him and his family her whole life.

"It's a good thing your boyfriend was here to intercept that lunatic," Liv said. "Who knows what he might have done?"

Heather froze. Remembering the pulse of attraction last night as she'd tended to Tyler's chin, Heather's face flamed. She should have known Liv wouldn't believe her when she insisted she and Tyler weren't romantically involved. "Tyler is not my boyfriend, but, yes, it was good that he was here." Confusion swirled through her. Had Ernesto been the one to call her the other night, advising her to leave the farm? "Ernesto and his brother, Sal, have been with the farm for longer than I can remember. He was trying to warn me, not threaten me."

"Right. You believed him?" Liv flicked her blond hair. "That whole bit about bad people and not trusting anyone was probably his way of weaseling out of a breaking and entering charge."

At one time, Heather might have agreed, but with all that had happened, she knew the man hadn't been fabricating a plausible excuse. He knew something. Something about the drugs and Seth's death. Heather had confidence that Tyler would find out exactly what. In the meantime, Heather's job was to keep Liv and Colin in the dark about the danger. She didn't want to upset either one of them. Liv's grief was still so raw, and Colin was too young to be burdened with the truth.

Heather glanced at the wall clock. It was a quarter after eight in the morning. "The sheriff will be here soon," Heather pointed out, gesturing to Liv's silky pink robe over the matching nightgown. She hoped Liv would get the hint that she needed to change out of her pajamas. Heather had pulled on sweats when she'd heard the commotion, and though she wasn't dressed fashionably, she was presentable. But she did need to do something with her hair and brush her teeth.

Liv's eyes widened, and she let out a little yelp of dismay. "I better change." She hurried out of the living room and down the hall, disappearing into Seth's room.

Heather took the opportunity to duck out the front door. Ernesto sat on the stairs, his head in his hands. Tyler, Blake and Nathanial conversed a few feet away. Taking advantage of the moment, Heather sat down beside Ernesto.

"Ernesto, who are the bad people?"

His head snapped up. His dark eyes grew round. "Oh, Mrs. Randall, I'm so sorry. I don't know what I was thinking to come here like this. I meant no harm."

She smiled at him, willing him to stop dodging her question. "I'm sure you didn't. But what did you mean?"

"No, no. I am drunk." He smiled crookedly. "I need to go to jail."

"Are you the one who called me the other night telling me to leave the farm?"

He shook his head. The pleading expression in his gaze tugged at her. "Not me, but that's good advice. You should leave before something bad happens."

"What do you know about Seth's death?" she pressed in frustration.

The sound of a siren sent birds flying from the perfectly conical sheared Douglas fir trees closest to the snow-covered lawn.

Ernesto lurched to his feet and practically ran to the sheriff before the man had even brought his silver SUV to a halt. Tyler strode over to the vehicle as the sheriff got out. The three men conversed, and then the sheriff opened the back door for Ernesto to climb inside the vehicle. Heather watched the sheriff and Ernesto drive away with annoyance pounding at her temples. She hoped Tyler had been able to extract some information from Ernesto. She'd failed miserably convincing him to talk.

She approached Tyler where he stood with Blake and Nathanial. When she stopped beside Tyler, the other two men strode away.

"Well, what did Ernesto tell you?"

Tyler shook his head. "Nothing other than he wanted to go to jail. He said he'd be safe there."

A fissure of fear bubbled to the surface. "That doesn't sound good. He wouldn't answer my questions. This is all so...so... Argh."

She couldn't find words to express how upsetting and irritating and frightening this situation was for her. She'd come to the farm hoping, needing, a peaceful place to raise her son. There was nothing peaceful about having her brother murdered, drugs planted inside her Christmas trees, threats and warnings, people sneaking around at night. It was as if she'd stepped into a horror flick. At least there weren't psychos running around with chain saws. Though, she supposed that was possible because there were several chain saws on the farm. She shivered at the thought.

Cupping her elbow, Tyler urged her back to the house. "No, it doesn't sound good. Nothing about this sounds good."

Liv came out of the house as they reached the top step. She was dressed in dark skinny jeans tucked into her tall black boots and her pink coat was buttoned up. She slung her purse over her shoulder and held her phone in her right hand. Clearly she planned to leave.

"Where are you going?" Heather paused on the stairs with Tyler beside her. She didn't recall Liv saying she had somewhere to be on Thanksgiving.

Wrinkling her nose, Liv said, "I completely forgot I'd promised one of my clients I'd do her hair in an updo for her family Thanksgiving dinner." Liv hurried down the steps. "I'll stop by the grocery store on the way back and pick up a few things we're missing for our feast."

The thought of Liv's extravagant tastes sent a shudder through Heather. "There's something we need to talk about," Heather blurted. She didn't want to burden Liv with the sad state of the farm's finances, but she also didn't want Liv spending money when she may need to be saving it for herself.

Liv halted and spun around, sending her loose blond hair swirling. Cocking her head, she blinked at Heather. "Can it wait?"

Heather chewed the inside of her lip. Guilt ate at her for not being able to spit out what she needed to say.

"You can do this." Tyler leaned in close and whispered in her ear. "She's an adult. She can handle it."

Freaked out by the fact that he could tell what she was thinking, she slanted him a glance. He arched an eyebrow. *Okay.* Shaking off his uncanny ability to read her mind, Heather walked back down the stairs and gathered Liv's free hand in hers. "I don't want you spending your money on the farm."

A crease appeared between Liv's eyebrows. She opened her mouth to undoubtedly protest, but Heather rushed on to say, "Seth wasn't managing the farm's money well. He used the farm's income that should have been for paying bills to buy personal items."

At least Seth had been responsible enough to make payroll. Heather hadn't taken a salary from the farm, since she had no part in running the business. She'd assumed it would be her retirement nest egg.

Liv convulsed as if Heather had sent a bolt of electricity through her. "What are you saying?"

Though Heather had to get the issue out into the open, she still cringed as she explained. "Seth used funds that weren't his to buy your car. And the down payment on the town house…"

For a moment Heather feared Liv would either pass out or get sick. Her eyes went wide, her jaw dropped open.

Liv lifted their joined hands. Her diamond ring glinted in the sunlight. "This, too?"

With everything in her, Heather wanted to say no and let Liv keep the memento of Seth's love, but she couldn't lie to her. "I'm afraid so."

Liv pulled free of Heather's hand and slipped the ring off her finger. She handed the gold-and-diamond engagement ring to Heather. Her hand shook; her face paled. "Here. I can't do anything about the car or the town house right now, but next week…"

Tears burned the backs of Heather's eyes. She hated hurting Liv like this. But this was Seth's fault. A simmering anger boiled inside. "That will be soon enough."

She held the ring out. "If you want to wear this until next week, you can."

Liv's sad smile wobbled. "No. I would have to take it off eventually. Might as well be today." With a small cry of distress, she hurried to where she'd parked her new luxury sedan and drove away.

Heather clutched the ring in her hand and pressed her fist against her heart. "Oh, Seth. You hurt so many people."

Sensing Tyler behind her, she didn't resist when he put his arms around her and pulled her close. She needed his strength at the moment. Her throat worked, but she couldn't thank him.

Slowly, he turned her to face him. With his hands on her shoulders, he dipped his head to meet her gaze. "You did the right thing by telling her."

"I know." She sighed. "But it doesn't make it hurt any less."

He rubbed her arms. "We have a Thanksgiving feast to get ready."

She appreciated his attempt to distract her. "Yes. We do." She stepped back and regained her composure. "I'm going to wake Colin and get him ready." She slipped the ring in her pocket. "Then we'll have to grab tables and chairs out of the barn's attic."

A loud explosion rent the air. The earth shook.

Startled, Heather jumped and collided with Tyler. He held her tightly against him. She grabbed his arm as an anchor as her mind tried to make sense of what was happening. A black plume of smoke billowed from behind the building that housed the farm's machinery.

Stricken, she met Tyler's gaze. "Oh, no! The propane tank!"

Flames shot toward the sky. Even though the wave

of heat made sweat break out on her brow, the dawning horror sweeping through her froze her blood. "There are gas tanks inside the building. If the fire reaches it—"

She broke free of Tyler's arms and ran toward the fire.

Tyler caught her about the waist and hauled her off her feet. "No." He swung around to face the house and carried her to the porch.

Beating at his arms, she cried, "We have to move the equipment out."

"Someone will." He set her down but kept a firm hand on her arm. "But not you."

His cell phone buzzed. He yanked it from his pants pocket. "Yeah?…I see it. I'll call nine-one-one. Heather says there are gas tanks inside the building…Roger that." He clicked off, then dialed the emergency number and quickly explained the situation. When he hung up, he turned his grim gaze on Heather. "Blake and Nathanial will do what they can to keep the fire contained until the fire department arrives."

"This wasn't an accident, was it?"

"I seriously doubt it."

Her hands fisted. "We should help them."

"It's too dangerous. I promised you I wouldn't let anything happen to you or Colin, and I mean to keep that promise."

She shook her head. "But you can't make that kind of promise." Her gaze went to the rising black smoke. "Bad things happen despite how much we pray and hope they won't." Tears blurred her vision. "Ken promised he'd come home, but he couldn't have predicted his helicopter would crash." She turned her gaze to Tyler. "Any more than you can guarantee whoever is trying to hurt the farm, hurt me, won't succeed. Life is random. Unpredictable. And scary."

Taking her in his arms, he held her close. His heart beat a frantic tune in her ear. "You're right. I can't anticipate every scenario, control every moment, but I can promise I will do everything humanly possible to keep you and Colin safe. The rest I have to trust to God."

His words reverberated through her. Trusting God. She did. But yet there was a small part of her that held back. Anger reared up, demanding to be acknowledged. "I'm so mad. Mad at Seth. Mad at the person doing this. Mad at God."

But not Tyler. She'd let go of her initial anger at him for using Seth because ultimately the responsibility of all this lay on Seth. And he'd paid a steep price for his actions.

Tyler pulled back to look into her face. "It's okay to be mad, but your feelings shouldn't dictate your trust of God. God is the same yesterday, today and tomorrow. His love and faithfulness never changes."

She really wanted to believe him. But at the moment it felt as though God were far away.

Behind her, the front door opened and Colin raced out to latch onto her leg. "Mommy? What's happening?"

She disentangled herself from Tyler and bent to pick up Colin. "Something caught on fire."

As her employees raced to help, she did a mental head count to make sure everyone was accounted for. Thankfully everyone was.

It seemed like an eternity before the distinct sound of a fire engine approaching drew her attention. "Hurry, hurry," she muttered.

Colin pointed toward the drive. "Look, a fire truck."

Hugging her son close, Heather was grateful Colin was more interested in the truck than the fire.

The three of them watched the six firemen disappear behind the building to extinguish the flames. Colin was awed by the whole process. Heather had to admit she was pretty wowed, as well. She had no idea they used foam to put out this kind of gas fire. She'd never seen firefighters in action in real life. While some of the firemen worked at extinguishing the propane fire, others hosed down the outside wall of the machinery building with water to keep the building cool so there'd be no secondary fires. When the fire was finally out, Heather, Tyler and Colin thanked the firemen. The captain even let Colin climb inside the truck and sit behind the wheel.

Blake and Nathanial joined Tyler and Heather. Both men were covered with soot, their faces streaked with black ashes.

"The fire investigator will be here later to take a look at the scene," the captain told them. His curious gaze landed on Blake and Nathanial. "You two did a good job of isolating the flames."

The two men looked almost embarrassed. Heather hid a grin. She was thankful she could smile now that the catastrophe had been averted. Though the air still reeked of the residual propane that had burned and smoke created a haze that she hoped would dissipate by tomorrow when they opened for business. Fortunately, the Christmas Village was on the far side of the property and was accessed by a different entrance.

"Captain, would you and your men like to stay for Thanksgiving dinner?"

"That's kind of you to offer, Mrs. Randall, but we're set with our own feast waiting back at the station house," he replied, then plopped his hat on his head. "Happy

Thanksgiving." He held up a finger and made a circular motion. "Let's round up and hit the road."

The six firefighters climbed aboard the truck and waved as the red engine backed out of the driveway and then drove away, back to Bonners Ferry.

As soon as the truck was out of sight, Heather looked at Blake and Nathanial. "Thank you both for...everything."

"Just doing our job," Blake stated with a cryptic look at Tyler.

Nathanial flashed a grin. "We weren't going to let a fire ruin our feast."

"Speaking of which," Heather said. "I can take it from here. You need to clean up and meet back here at two. We'll eat at three."

Blake gave a single nod before turning on his work boot heel and striding away.

Nathanial shook his head at his coworker's retreating back. "He's not one for too many words." He smiled again at Heather. "We'll be back to help set up." He saluted Tyler, then jogged away to catch up to Blake.

Heather caught Tyler's gaze. "I don't know what I would have done if you and your team hadn't shown up when you did."

For that she would thank God every day. Even when Tyler left, she'd know she'd been changed by his presence. For the better.

Tyler was so proud of the way Heather managed to keep a positive attitude as she tirelessly served the twelve men in her employ who didn't have family in the area to go to for the holiday meal. Ernesto wasn't among them. Nor did he recognize the face of the man he'd wrestled with last night. The one wearing the ring Tyler's face had become well acquainted with.

They'd set up another long table connecting end to end with the farmhouse's dining room table. The turkey was moist and delicious, the side dishes mouthwatering and the pumpkin pie sweet. After the excitement of the fire, which Liv seemed convinced was a terrible accident, everyone, including Blake, Nathanial and Liv, seemed to be having a good time. Conversations and banter filled the house. Colin couldn't sit still. He bounced from person to person, retelling how the firefighters had put out the flames and declaring he wanted to be a firefighter when he grew up.

Sitting back, watching the festivities, Tyler knew a contentment he'd never experienced before. To be a part of a family-type gathering was something new for him. Oh, his grandparents had tried to make the few holidays he'd been able to spend with them homey, but it hadn't been like this, noisy and festive and full of cheer. His grandparents had been somber people with quiet voices, but they had been filled with love for each other. And love for Tyler.

As an adult he always volunteered for an assignment on Thanksgiving and Christmas. Better to let those with families have the time off. He'd never minded missing out on something he never had to begin with. But he was glad that today he hadn't had to miss out. This could be his one and only opportunity to experience a real family-style Thanksgiving feast with people he would like to call friends.

That was, if he weren't so aware that besides his team members, Heather, Liv and Colin, any one of the others could be involved in murder and part of a drug ring. Kind of put a damper on things. But for the moment,

Heather and Colin were safe and clearly enjoying themselves. He'd take it. As a memory to cherish.

Colin climbed onto Tyler's lap. "Mr. Tyler, what are you thankful for?"

Tyler tweaked the boy's nose. "I'm thankful for Christmas trees."

A big grin spread over Colin's face. "Me, too!" He rubbed his hands together. "I can't wait for Christmas."

"Hear, hear," someone said.

Tyler met Heather's gaze over the top of Colin's head. The gentle affection in her eyes and the small pleased smile playing at the corner of her mouth hit him like a ton of bricks. Momentarily stunned, he realized the war within himself to keep his defenses from crumbling was in full battle mode. Uneasy concern slipped into his psyche like a sliver festering beneath a fingernail. Yet he found he didn't want to fight it. He wanted to embrace this new and wonderful occurrence.

Blake scooted his chair away from the table and cleared his throat. Tyler's focus snapped to him. Blake jerked his head toward the door before he left the table and exited the room.

Nathanial scooped up a roll and popped it into his mouth before following Blake.

Tyler sighed, reining in the wayward emotions that would only lead down a path he really had no business traveling. The fun and games were over. Time for Blake to leave with the truck full of trees stashed with cocaine.

Setting Colin back on the floor, Tyler ruffled the boy's hair. "Gotta see Blake off."

Heather came over and took Colin's hand. "Come on, sweetie. Time to start cleaning up."

At her cue, the men rose, clearing their plates and the serving dishes from the tables.

"Colin, let's wash the dishes together," Liv called from the doorway to the kitchen.

Heather let go of his hand. Colin ran to help Liv.

"He's a great kid," Tyler told her as they moved to the entryway. "You've done such a good job with him."

She beamed. "He is great." Her smile dimmed, and she lowered her voice. "So it begins?"

He knew she referred to the sting operation that the IBETs were orchestrating on the tree farm in Canada that would be receiving the illegal drugs. That was if the trees cleared customs. Seeing how well they'd hidden the drugs and concealed the scent, Tyler didn't doubt the truck would be waved through this time. But after that, never again. The IBETs director would make sure every border crossing was aware of the sneaky way the drugs were being smuggled.

Rob hobbled over to join them. "It's fortuitous of your friend to have family up north. I appreciate him volunteering to drive the truck across the border."

Wary of Rob's intentions, Tyler shrugged. "Yes, it is."

"Is it his parents that live near Calgary?"

Remembering the cover story they'd devised, Tyler shook his head. "No. Cousins."

Rob raised his eyebrows. "Ah, right."

"Rob, would you mind going over tomorrow's schedule with me one more time?" Heather asked, drawing the older man's attention away from Tyler.

Bless her. Tyler would have to thank her later for giving him the perfect opportunity to slip out the door.

Blake and Nathanial were waiting at the edge of the driveway.

"Everything is in place," Blake said. "Border Patrol agent Jeff Steele is meeting me at the Eastport–Kingsgate crossing."

"Good." Tyler liked Steele. He was a stand-up guy. They'd worked together on a few assignments. Though Tyler hadn't been on the assignment where Steele had met his wife, Dr. Tessa Cleary, Tyler had met the red-headed fish biologist at their wedding. He'd liked her. And Tyler had to admit he'd been slightly envious.

The thought of having someone to spend the rest of his life with tied Tyler up in knots. An image of Heather danced through his mind, and his mouth went dry. The battle he'd been fighting seemed to lean toward disaster. He was in real jeopardy of falling hard for this woman.

He gave himself a mental shake to dislodge the image. Not meant for him. What did he have to offer Heather and Colin? Nothing. With determination, he told himself to stop longing for what would never be and put his mind on the job that needed to be finished.

ELEVEN

After the Thanksgiving dishes were cleaned and put away, and the guests had dispersed, Heather took a moment to sit down on the couch with Colin tucked beside her in the same position she'd seen Tyler with Colin earlier.

Seeing them together had brought an ache of loss for all that Ken had missed and for Colin not knowing his father. And for what couldn't be with Tyler.

He'd made it clear he wanted no part of being a family. He'd made the statement he wasn't father material, but he was so wrong. He related well to Colin, playing with and teasing her son. Encouraging him on his trike and being content to sit with Colin watching a kids' show. Tyler would be an excellent father.

She wished she could tell him that, but she wouldn't. She wouldn't make his eventual leaving any more difficult by pointing out that he wasn't being honest with himself. That denying his own abilities and worth was keeping him from potentially finding the beauty of a family. Of love.

Not that she'd fallen for him.

Okay, maybe a bit, if she was honest with herself.

But she couldn't let affection for him make her vulnerable to hurt, not if she hoped to survive his leaving.

Liv came into the room carrying a mug. "I made you a cup of tea."

"Thank you." Heather accepted the cup and wrapped her hands around it, letting the heat warm her. The calming scent of chamomile rose with the steam. She took a sip, warm but not too hot to drink. It felt good going down, but after a bit she realized the tea didn't agree with her tummy.

She set the half-empty mug on the coffee table. She was obviously too upset to drink anything. She'd barely eaten as it was, and the little she did manage to get down hadn't wanted to stay down. All the stress lately had really done a number on her digestion.

A few minutes later, Liv returned to the living room and sat on the recliner. She had a small leather book in her hands.

Heather's heart bumped against her ribs. Was that Seth's journal? "Liv, what do you have there?"

Liv held it up with a sad smile. "I found this in one of the boxes Seth had moved into the town house's garage."

Heather's mouth went dry. She placed a hand over her roiling stomach. "Have you read it?"

Liv shook her head. "Just the first page." Tears gathered in her eyes. "I couldn't bring myself to read any more."

Needing to get the book to Tyler, Heather extracted herself from Colin and rose. For a moment the room tilted. She braced her feet apart, chiding herself for getting up too quickly.

Colin jumped to his feet. "Mommy, can I have a snack?"

"Of course."

Colin raced into the kitchen.

As Heather made her way to Liv's side, she struggled to keep the dizziness from overcoming her. She didn't have a cold, so she wasn't sure why her equilibrium was off. "May I see the book?"

Liv handed the notebook over. "If you discover why he—" she lowered her voice to a whisper "—started using again, you'll let me know?"

Grateful for her consideration of Colin, Heather touched Liv's shoulder. "Of course."

Liv's mouth twisted. "I hope it wasn't because of me."

Seeing the hurt on Liv's face, Heather crouched down and took her hand. "Liv, you aren't to blame. Seth loved you. His death—" She clamped her lips together to keep from spilling out the truth.

Once Tyler arrested the person responsible for Seth's death, then Heather would reveal the whole story to Liv. But until then it would be wiser, safer, to keep Liv in the dark. "Please, don't think that you had anything to do with his death."

"I keep wondering if I wasn't enough for him." She darted a glance at Colin as he skipped back into the living room with a bowl of animal crackers. Liv's face softened with love, but her eyes were sad as she looked back at Heather. "I was so looking forward to being a part of your family."

"You'll always be a part of our lives," Heather assured her and meant it. Spending this time with Liv had given Heather a chance to get to know her better. Heather liked how generous and caring Liv was to both her and Colin. Which only made the loss of Liv becoming Heather's sister-in-law more distressing.

Liv squeezed her hand. "Thank you for saying so."

She released Heather's hand and stood. "I'm going to go lie down. It's been an emotional day."

Heather understood the feeling. She'd like nothing more than to crawl beneath her covers and forget the past few weeks. But hiding from reality wasn't her style. With the notebook in hand, she went to the kitchen and called Tyler.

He answered on the first ring.

"Are you okay?" he asked.

She leaned on the counter. For some reason her legs were wobbly. Her head had stopped spinning though. That was good. "Yes. Liv found a small journal in Seth's things at the town house."

"I'll be right over," he said and hung up.

Heather waited for him at the back door. When she heard his boots on the stairs, she opened the door. "Blake and the truck are gone?"

"Yes. I was headed over here when you called."

His grim expression caused a riot of anxiety inside her. "What's wrong?"

"The other truck is missing."

"How can that be?" She knew Tyler had held on to the keys for both trucks and replaced the padlock on the refrigerated boxes.

"Someone else had a set of keys."

She groaned. "Seth's missing keys."

He nodded. "The new padlock had been cut off by bolt cutters."

Her stomach sank. "That's weird. Why would someone take an empty truck?"

"No clue. Though I plan to question Rob and Don. See if either of them have an explanation for the missing truck. Last I'd heard the trip east had been canceled."

She wanted to come to her employees' defense, but

she just couldn't be sure of their innocence. Ernesto's warning not to trust anyone rang through her mind.

"But the good news is we'd set up a surveillance camera," Tyler informed her. "I've sent the picture of the guy who stole the truck to my boss. He'll run it and see if we can get an ID on him. Thankfully he's not one of your employees. He doesn't match any of the IDs we have already on file. And all law enforcement agencies will be looking for the truck." He gestured to the book in her hands. "That's the notebook?"

She handed it to him. "I haven't looked at it. I wanted to wait for you."

"Let's sit, and we can read it together," he said.

After checking that Colin was occupied with one of his favorite animated movies, Heather and Tyler sat at the dining table. Tyler cracked the book open.

Heather read the date of the first entry with surprise. "He started this when he was in high school."

They flipped through the pages. As Heather read the words written in her brother's neat and precise hand-writing, sadness descended on her like a heavy cloak. The picture unfolding on the pages chronicled Seth's downward spiral into drugs. He'd started using to fit in with a certain crowd of kids. Kids he felt accepted him for who he was, which didn't make sense to Heather. If he'd felt the need to adopt a drug habit to fit in, then those kids hadn't truly accepted him. Acceptance came with no conditions. She wished she'd been around to explain that to him.

The deeper they went in the book, the sadder and angrier Heather became. Seth talked about the drugs and his dependence on them. He talked of the rehab centers their parents had dragged him to. If only he'd been able to get clean and stay clean. It wasn't until after their parents' fatal car accident that he'd been able to conquer the addiction.

He talked of meeting Liv in his last rehab center. Stunned, Heather met Tyler's gaze. "I didn't know that she had an addiction."

Tyler's eyes were soft with compassion. "Seth writes that she successfully kicked her habit. He clearly admired and respected her as well as loved her."

Grief ravaged Heather's heart. "Liv needs to read this. She thinks maybe he started using again because of her." Heather lowered her voice. "It was all I could do not to tell her the truth."

Tyler covered her hand with his. "You'll be able to soon."

Taking comfort from his touch, she continued to read. The words on the pages didn't make sense. Seth wrote that he felt guilty for their parents' death. Why? Farther down the page she had her answer. She read the entry with dawning horror.

Seth had been driving the car. He'd caused the accident that had taken her parents' lives. "No. This can't be true."

"You didn't know?"

Tyler's question pierced her to the quick. "No. Seth never said a word. I never dug into the accident. I took what I was told at face value. Dad lost control of the car and hit a tree, killing them both."

"There's nothing about it in the police report," Tyler admitted softly.

Her vision was blurry with tears. "You read the police report?"

"As part of my investigation. The report cited your dad as the driver. Seth had pulled your parents out of the car before emergency vehicles could arrive."

"So Seth lied to the police, too." She pinched the bridge of her nose. When would this madness end?

"If what he writes here is true, then, yes, he did."

"How could this happen?" She spread her hands out. "What made Seth into this person?" Blame clawed at her throat. "I let him down. I let my parents down. If I'd been a better sister—"

"No."

The sharpness in Tyler's tone startled her.

"You are not at fault for your brother's choices. He was an adult, capable of knowing right from wrong. As much as you'd like to believe you're in control, you're not. Only God has that kind of power, but He gives each of us free will to decide our own fates."

Tyler touched her cheek, his fingers so gentle and warm. Tears filled her eyes. He was right, of course. Berating herself for something she had no control over was a waste of time and energy. She wasn't a martyr. Releasing the burden of regret that she hadn't been there to help her brother and her parents wouldn't come easily, but acknowledging the need to was a start.

She forced back her tears. Her gaze dropped to the book. She didn't want to read any more about Seth and his lies. She wanted to know about the drugs. Nothing mattered except making the farm safe for Colin. For herself.

Flipping through the pages, she skimmed the words for anything that would tell them who on the farm was responsible for the drug trafficking. But there was nothing. The journal ended without providing any clues.

"Ugh!" She slammed the book shut. "This is useless."

Tyler put his hand on her shoulder. "Heather, we'll find the right notebook. It has to be here on the farm somewhere."

"But where?"

"We haven't completed our search of the village."

"True." There was still a chance they would find the incriminating evidence Tyler would need to bring down the drug smugglers and put an end to her brother's deceit. And then Tyler would no longer have a reason to stay.

There was nothing she could do about the fact that Tyler was leaving.

The next morning, Tyler stood at Heather's back door. She'd invited him for breakfast with her, Colin and Liv before heading over to the Christmas Village to open for the public. As an added precaution, Tyler had arranged for a couple of sheriff's deputies to have a presence at the village today. Tyler and the guys could have eyes on every person and every nook and cranny, so the added security for Heather and Colin was more than welcome. Last night, after the disappointment of realizing that the notebook Liv had found wasn't the one they needed, he and Heather had made a plan to spend the day in the village and covertly search for Seth's missing journal.

He could only imagine how shocking it had been for Heather to learn the truth that Seth had been the one driving when their parents were killed. It had taken all Tyler's self-control not to pull her into his arms.

He wanted to soothe her hurt, protect her from the painful reality that her brother hadn't been the man she'd thought he was. Instead of an embrace, he'd settled for touching her shoulder.

Even that simple, innocent touch created sparks and fueled his yearning to be the one to comfort her. As more than an assignment. As more than a friend.

What was wrong with him?

He knew better than to become emotionally involved. *Right.* He mentally snorted. His head may know, but his heart wasn't cooperating. Time to backpedal and gain some much-needed distance. Both physically and emotionally.

He turned to go, and the door opened.

"Mr. Tyler!" Colin ran full speed at him.

Tyler caught the child and lifted him high in the air. Colin's laugh settled in Tyler's chest. Tyler realized with a heavy sigh he would miss the boy. Setting Colin back on his feet, Tyler found Heather watching him with a look that made emotion clog his throat. There was tenderness in her gaze but also resignation, as if she, too, were aware how brief this time together would be.

Despite his mental lashing for letting his emotions off leash, it made him sad to think of the day when he'd no longer be at the farm. But he wanted that day to come because it would mean Heather and Colin were no longer in danger. There was no room for sentiment here. Only action.

"Eggs?" Liv called from where she stood at the stove.

Though he had no appetite—his stomach was tied up in knots from his conflicting thoughts—he nodded. It would be out of character and draw unwanted attention if he refused. He only wished he could hide the truth from himself as easily. "Please. Thank you."

Colin climbed off a chair at the table and dragged the chair next to him closer. "Sit here, Mr. Tyler."

Unable to refuse the kid, Tyler sat down. Heather brought over a mug of coffee for him. "Thank you."

She smiled, though her eyes didn't sparkle. He missed seeing the sparkle.

"You're welcome," Heather managed to say without

her voice trembling with suppressed emotions. "As soon as we're done with breakfast, we need to hurry to the village. The gate opens at nine."

That gave them a little under an hour to eat and hoof it across the property.

After they ate and cleaned up the breakfast dishes, Liv announced she was going into town. "I have clients," she explained before heading out the door.

Once Heather had Colin dressed and ready to go, they made the trek to the Christmas Village, which was abuzz with activity. She was grateful to see two of Boundary County's sheriff deputies walking around, keeping an eye on things. Tyler had mentioned he'd asked for the help. She hoped their day was quiet and boring.

She waved to Deputy Daniel Potter. They'd gone to high school together. He nodded a greeting.

The Thanksgiving snowstorm had left a nice layer of white powder on the rooftops, but the sidewalks had been cleared. The graveled lot in the middle of the village showed faint tracks of the large gold-gilded horse-drawn sleigh that waited near the bakery. A man dressed in a Santa suit stood in front of a building labeled Santa's House and waved at them.

"Santa!" Colin cried and ran for the man.

"That's Don," Heather explained.

"Now's a good time to ask about the missing truck."

Heather shielded her eyes from the morning sun as they strode over to where the bearded man in the red suit had bent down to hand Colin a candy cane.

When Don straightened, Heather put her hand on her son's shoulder. Noticing Deputy Potter, she waved him over and introduced him to Tyler, Don and Colin.

"Daniel and I were in the same grade growing up. He married one of my high school friends."

Daniel grinned at her. "Betsy says hi. She and the kids are planning to come out on Sunday after church."

"Wonderful." Sensing Tyler's impatience to talk to Don, Heather said, "Colin, do you want to see if Mrs. Theid needs more help?"

"Yes!"

Daniel stepped forward. "Would you like me to take him to the bakery?"

Grateful for the offer, she said, "That would be fabulous. Thank you."

"Sure thing." Daniel directed his attention to Colin. "Lead the way, young man."

"Thanks, Santa, for the candy cane." Colin raced away, and Daniel hurried after him.

Heather appreciated that Colin had his own deputy sheriff watching over him.

As soon as Colin was out of earshot, Tyler faced Don. "One of the refrigerated trucks went missing last night. What do you know about that?"

Behind his white bead, Don frowned. "It's not missing. The truck headed east to bring back a load of imported trees from Canada's northeast region." He turned his gaze to Heather. "Didn't Seth tell you this?"

Heather frowned. "I knew the truck was headed east, but since trees were never loaded into it, I assumed that meant it wasn't going to be used. Seth never mentioned anything about importing trees." Of course there seemed to be a great number of things her brother had neglected to share with her. So why was she surprised? "When did this start?"

"We tried it last year as an experiment," Don answered. "And it went so well that Seth had arranged for another load this year."

"Why would you import trees when you grow trees?" Tyler asked. The whole thing sounded suspicious.

"Because we don't grow balsam fir, which is pretty popular, as it turns out. I think it's the novelty of having something different." Don shrugged. "The balsams grow in the northeastern part of the United States and Canada. Seth found a grower willing to bring the trees halfway. The trees in the shipment coming in are already spoken for. When the truck rolls back in on Saturday, there will be a line of folks coming from as far away as California waiting to pick up their tree."

That definitely set Tyler's senses on alert. He'd make sure to get a look at the trees that came back. "Can you get me the contact info for the supplier of these balsam trees?"

"Sure. I won't have time until noon when I take my lunch." Don's gaze moved past them to the front gate. "Oops," he said. "I better get to my post. It looks like the gate's opening."

"Thank you, Don," Heather said. When he'd gone inside, she turned to Tyler. "I need to check on Colin and then the front to make sure everything is running smoothly." She shook her head with self-mockery. "I shouldn't worry. Everyone here knows what they're doing."

"It's okay to be concerned, considering what's happened this week." Tyler didn't blame Heather for expecting the worst. One of these people could potentially be Seth's killer. And was definitely involved with the illegal drugs stuffed inside the Christmas trees headed to Calgary.

At the bakery, they found Colin wearing a small

apron and kneading pastry dough. Mrs. Theid was in the process of putting out a batch of warm scones and cinnamon rolls in the display case. Deputy Potter had taken up a position near the door where he could keep an eye on Colin and on the activities outside.

Heather put her hand to the mouth. Her face had gone white.

Concerned, he touched her elbow. "Are you okay?"

"I need fresh air." She hurried outside.

Tyler followed her. She gulped air as if she were oxygen deprived.

"What's going on?"

"The smell of the grease was too much for me," she explained.

The only aroma he'd smelled was the cinnamon rolls.

They walked to the front gate where Rob oversaw the admittance box. A line had formed of people eager to come and see the Christmas Village. Heather asked if the attendants needed anything. They assured her they had everything under control.

"Come on," she said to Tyler. "Let's pretend for a few moments we're tourists."

He smiled, glad to see the color back in her pretty face. "Okay. Take me on a tour of the village."

She led him through the gift shop, where they sold handcrafted items from local artisans as well as an assortment of different types of ornaments. Christmas carols played from speakers mounted in the corner. Heather sang along for a moment, her voice clear and melodic. She encouraged him to sing, so he added his baritone voice to hers. Their two voices melded well together. They were compatible in so many ways. He shook off the wayward thought and stopped singing.

"I doubt Seth would hide the journal in a place where

it could be accidentally found by anyone in the shop," he whispered to Heather.

With a nod, she thanked the carolers. She and Tyler moved on to the train depot, where a modular train set was on display. He enjoyed the excitement in Heather's tone as she explained how the set had been collected and built by her grandfather. Tyler had to force himself to remember why they were in the train depot building.

After covertly searching the building and not finding the notebook, they continued on their way. Heather linked her arm through his as they made their way down one side of the little make-believe town. Tyler couldn't stop himself from enjoying the closeness even as he began to despair they'd never find Seth's journal.

Plus, the place was now packed. Tyler hadn't expected the village to be so popular. Families, young couples, older couples all filed in to pass some time in the village, buying gifts in the gift shop, eating pastries or sipping hot cocoa, before heading to either the precut tree lot or to hike through the rows of trees to cut their own.

Keeping Heather close to his side, he moved through the crowds until they came to a stop outside a petting pen where the mannequin nativity scene was lighted from the back, making the figurines glow. Children petted the goats, sheep, a small donkey and some rabbits. The snow turned dirty beneath the animals' hoofs and children's feet.

"I don't remember rabbits in the story of baby Jesus's birth," he commented to Heather.

She laughed. "We make do with what we have. One year when I was a kid, my dad put ducks in the pen. He'd found them wandering on the property, so he cared for them and they stayed for a long time. Then one day they flew away."

He chuckled. "That must have been disappointing."

She shook her head. "They were free to go. But we decided it would be best to keep grounded animals from then on."

Staring into her beautiful eyes, Tyler felt grounded, anchored in a way he'd not thought possible.

"Tyler!" Nathanial waved them over to where he stood by the precut trees, which had been wrapped in plastic netting.

He was grateful for the excuse to dispel the disconcerting sensation. No matter how much he liked and admired and respected this woman, he eventually had to walk away. That was the nature of his job. The nature of his life.

They joined Nathanial. "What's up?" Tyler asked.

"I just heard from Blake. The sting was a bust."

Not the news Tyler wanted to hear. "What happened?"

"When they arrived at the location where they were to drop off the trees, they were told to take them back. They wouldn't take possession of them."

"Do you think they found out it was a sting?" Heather asked.

Tyler ran a hand through his hair. "If so, how? We've been careful here. I don't think anyone suspects we're law enforcement."

"Maybe, maybe not," Nathanial said. "I did overhear a couple of the guys talking about a shipment they were expecting. When I asked what they meant, they clammed up."

"We just learned that the missing truck isn't exactly missing," Tyler said. "A shipment of trees coming from the northeast part of Canada will be arriving sometime tomorrow. Don said he'd get me the info at noon."

Heather touched Tyler's arm. "It's a quarter to noon. I should get Colin back to the house for lunch and a nap."

"I'll escort you," Nathanial offered. "While Tyler talks with Don."

It was logical for the other man to take Heather and Colin back to the house and stay with them as protection, yet Tyler didn't want to let Heather out of his sight. But he couldn't very well protest. He had a job to do. It would be strange and suspicious for Nathanial to get the information from Don.

And right now, he had to focus on his job.

"As soon as I'm done talking with Don, I'll come back to the house," Tyler promised.

Heather smiled. "We'll be fine."

Of course they would be. Nathanial would keep them safe. As he watched them walk toward the bakery, Tyler couldn't deny he was falling for the beautiful widow despite knowing he shouldn't. He had nothing to offer her. Nothing but love.

He snorted. What did he know of love?

Nothing. Nothing at all. And he didn't see that changing anytime soon.

Heather had to pry Colin from the bakery. "Come on, sweetie. It's time to have lunch."

"But I'm not hungry, and I'm helping customers," Colin declared.

Bending down so they were eye to eye, Heather said, "Sweetheart, we are going now. If you want to come back this afternoon, you need to cooperate now. It's your choice."

His bottom lip stuck out. "Fine. I'll cooperate."

She took him by the hand, and they met Nathanial on the wooden sidewalk.

"I thought we'd ride back to the house in the truck," Nathanial said.

Grateful for his thoughtfulness, Heather smiled. "That's a good idea. I need to touch base with Rob first and let him know I'll be at the house if he needs anything."

They found Rob in Santa's House. He'd put on the Santa outfit so that Don could take a break. A line of children and parents waited along the sidewalk to get their pictures taken with Santa. Two women dressed in green elf costumes played Santa's helpers. One controlled the line while the other manned the camera.

Colin slipped inside and ran straight for Rob, beating out a little girl of about four.

Heather rushed to pluck Colin up and held him on her hip. "Honey, there's a line. You'll get your chance to have your picture taken with Santa later."

"Ah, man," Colin groused.

To Rob, Heather said, "I'm taking him to the house. If you need anything, call."

"You aren't going alone, are you?" Rob rose from the large chair.

Uneasy with his concern, she replied, "No. Nathanial is taking us over."

He settled back onto the chair. "Good. You shouldn't be alone."

Not sure what to make of his words, she turned to go and noticed the supply closet door had a shiny new padlock on it.

"Rob, when did you put the lock on the closet?"

"I didn't," he replied. "I thought you had."

"No, I didn't."

"Then Seth must have."

Could this be where he had hidden his journal? She remembered seeing a set of small keys in his desk drawer when she was searching his room for the notebook. Could those keys fit the padlock? Would they find the answers to his death behind the door?

She hurried from the building. She couldn't wait to tell Tyler.

TWELVE

"Finish your mac and cheese, sweetie. Then we can head back over to the village." Heather rose from the table with her own plate and took it to the sink. Through the window over the sink she saw Nathanial walk by. She'd invited him in for lunch, but the man had politely declined, saying he wanted to stand guard outside. Walking the perimeter, as Tyler had called it.

She smiled at the thought of Tyler. This morning, strolling through the Christmas Village together, arm in arm, had filled her with a serenity she hadn't felt in a long time. She had to fight against wishing the contentment would last. She had to stop letting herself hope for something with Tyler that wasn't going to happen. For now she'd appreciate his presence. His and his crew's, that was.

Admittedly, she was grateful for the time alone with her son. It seemed in the past few days there had been little opportunity for some one-on-one time with Colin. He'd talked nonstop from the moment they'd entered the house. It seemed he, too, was taken with Tyler and Nathanial. But what boy wouldn't be when he had no father figure in his life?

Maybe she was doing her son a disservice by not seeking companionship and love again.

The thought slid through her, stirring up yearnings she'd thought she'd suppressed. But only now did she realize they had been bubbling in her subconscious for days.

Yearnings for someone to share her burdens and her joys with. Someone to teach her son how to be a man. Someone to love and cherish her, to make her feel wanted and beautiful.

The way Tyler did.

But Tyler couldn't be that man. Even if she really wanted him to be. He didn't want a family. He was married to his job. End of story. And she needed to keep herself in check if she didn't want to end up brokenhearted when he left.

And the sooner they found Seth's journal, the sooner she could get on with her life. Alone. But safe.

After setting her dish in the dishwasher, she made a beeline for Seth's room. She knocked just in case Liv had returned, though Heather hadn't seen her car in the driveway. Hesitating for the briefest moment, she pushed open the door. After the break-in, she and Tyler had restored the room as much as they could, but it was still a blow to see the bed rumpled just like Seth would always leave his bed. But then Liv's clothes strewn over the chair in the corner and hanging in the closet reminded Heather that Seth was gone.

She hastened to the desk and paused as her attention landed on the stack of photos waiting to be attached to the large three-sided poster board that was now tucked away between the bed and the desk. The photo showed Seth mugging for the camera wearing a jersey with the Steelheads logo of the Idaho minor-league ice hockey team he followed. He'd loved the sport of ice hockey and had played for a while in his teens, but then drugs had put a damper on things and he'd quit.

"Oh, Seth." Heather heaved a disappointed, sad sigh that vibrated through her and made tears well.

Blinking quickly to rid herself of the waterworks, she opened the top dresser drawer. When she'd returned the contents after the intruder had dumped them on the floor, she hadn't take time to arrange anything, so she had to wade through the jumble of pens, paperclips, packs of chewing gum and other miscellaneous things that had found their way inside.

She found the two tiny keys she'd noticed earlier fastened together with a ring. She'd shut the drawer and turned to go when her gaze snagged on a small clear vial filled with white powder on the floor under the desk.

She picked it up. Was this cocaine? Had the intruder left it behind? Heather hadn't recalled seeing it when they had searched the room for the journal or when they'd cleaned up the mess left after the break-in. But maybe it was Seth's? Or had Liv brought this into Heather's house? Heather hated to even contemplate the idea. Was Liv using again? Had Seth's death led Liv back down a destructive path?

"Oh, please no, Lord." Unfortunately, she couldn't shake the thought that Liv was back to her old ways. Another more horrifying thought ricocheted through Heather's mind. Was Liv involved in the drug trafficking?

No. Heather refused to believe that Liv was complicit in something illegal. She had a thriving hair salon to protect. And she certainly wouldn't have killed Seth. She'd loved him too much. But that loss could have sent her running for something to dull the pain.

Tucking the petite bottle into her pocket, she left the room. She could be totally jumping to conclusions. Heather didn't know how to tell if the powder was cocaine or something less sinister. For all she knew, the vial could contain a sleep aid.

She'd ask Tyler and see what he thought. Later tonight she could broach the subject of the vial and its contents with Liv. And if the bottle was filled with cocaine, she'd hopefully be able to convince Liv not to destroy the life she'd built by using again. And Heather was sure Tyler would want to know who her supplier was.

Heather refused to believe the worst of Liv. Not when they were just starting to get to know each other.

When they were ready to leave the house, Nathanial drove them back to the Christmas Village.

"Can I go back to the bakery?" Colin hopped from foot to foot, clearly anxious to help Mrs. Theid again.

Heather had a feeling it was the free pastries and ice cream that he wanted. But she didn't want to burden Mrs. Theid, and she didn't like the idea of Colin not being protected.

"I'll ask the deputy to keep an eye on him," Nathanial offered, somehow sensing her hesitation.

How could she refuse? "I'm okay with you helping out Mrs. Theid, but only one treat."

His little face scrunched up in protest.

Heather arched an eyebrow.

Colin heaved a sigh that made his shoulders droop for a moment. "Fine. One treat." Then he was off, running for the bakery. Heather followed him while Nathanial found Deputy Potter and sent him to the bakery.

After thanking Daniel and making sure Colin wasn't bothering the baker, Heather took a turn at the front

gate for a couple of hours. A prickly current of aware-
ness announced Tyler's presence when he relived Nathanial as her shadow.

She put Tyler to work handing out the brochures and
giving directions to the trees. When there was a lull,
she grabbed the vial from her coat pocket and called to
Tyler. He stepped over, and she took his hand, slipping
the vial into his palm. "I found this in Seth's room."

He gave her a quizzical look. "When?"

"This morning."

She could see the questions churning in his eyes as
he tucked the vial into a pocket, but there was no time
for more conversation. The time passed quickly as more
visitors arrived and the excitement of the Christmas
season settled inside Heather. Despite the dangers, they
would soon be celebrating Jesus's birthday.

When the next person scheduled to man the entrance
arrived, Heather and Tyler made their way to the gift
shop, where she would relieve the woman behind the
counter.

Tyler patted the pocket where he'd stashed the vial.
"This wasn't in Seth's room when we searched it or
after the break-in. I would have noticed."

"I know," Heather admitted. "Do you think it's—"
she lowered her voice "—cocaine?"

"I won't know for sure until I test it." He opened the
gift shop door for her.

As she passed him, she said, "I hope it's not."

He nodded in understanding.

Heather settled behind the cash register. After about
ten minutes in the gift store, it was clear Tyler was uncomfortable as he fidgeted and tried to find a spot out of
the way among the ornaments and knickknacks. There
were a few scary moments when she thought he'd knock

over a display as he tried to stay out of the way of the customers. Taking pity on him, she said, "I'm fine." She held up her phone. "I have you on speed dial."

He gave her a lopsided grin that did funny things to her insides. "Thanks. I'll be right outside."

A few hours later, the gift shop quieted down. She'd ended up staying even after her employee returned because there were so many customers waiting to be helped. It was nearly closing time. She debated gathering Colin from the bakery but decided to wait a little longer when she spotted Tyler and Rob deep in conversation by the puppet playhouse. At the moment the puppets were gone, but the puppeteers did two shows a day, one in the morning and one in the afternoon. As a kid she'd been fascinated by the handmade puppets.

She stepped up, and the men stopped talking. "Sorry to interrupt."

"Not at all," Rob said. "We were just discussing the finer points of physical therapy."

She slanted her gaze to Tyler. "I didn't know you'd ever had PT." In fact there was a great deal she didn't know about Tyler. And wouldn't learn because they weren't in a relationship. A stab of regret reverberated through her, but she steadfastly ignored it. She had to remember that there was no future for her and Tyler.

"I was stabbed with a hunting knife in the thigh a few years ago," Tyler explained. "Thankfully, no arteries were nicked, and the blade missed the bone. But it took a good six months before I was able to walk without limping. But my PT wasn't nearly as involved as Rob's."

She wondered if the incident had occurred while he was on the job. Most likely. "You were fortunate." So was Rob, but she could never bring herself to broach the topic of the tragedy that had taken his family and left him scarred.

Tyler's cell phone rang. "Excuse me." He walked a few paces away as he answered.

Heather watched him for a moment. She'd known he had a dangerous job, but for some reason the reality hadn't sunk in until now. What was it about alpha males willing to put their own lives at risk for others that drew her in like a bee to a picnic? The thought knocked her back a step. Ken's job had been dangerous just like Tyler's. The connection couldn't be ignored. And one more reason why she couldn't let herself fully fall for the handsome DEA agent. She never wanted to go through that kind of loss again.

"You like him," Rob stated, his voice gruff.

Yes. She couldn't lie to herself. She more than liked Tyler. Alarm fluttered through her.

But she was unwilling to engage in a conversation with Rob about her affection for the DEA agent. Instead she held up the two keys. "Let's see if these fit the padlock."

Rob inclined his head. "After you."

She motioned to Tyler, letting him know where she was going, then walked with purpose to Santa's House. The line had thinned; she'd bring Colin over for his picture with Santa after looking in the supply closet to see if Seth's journal was hidden there.

She and Rob slipped inside the house. Thankfully, the big chair Santa sat in hid her and Rob from the camera's lens as the last of the visitors had their picture taken with Santa. She fit the tiny key in the lock. It worked.

Pleased, she undid the padlock and cracked open the door to peer inside. The interior was dark. She groped for the chain that would turn on the single overhead light. Her finger curled around the chain and she tugged. Light dispersed the shadows. The closet had been emptied of the supplies it was supposed to hold. Instead, there was a small desk and a chair. A black book sat on the desk.

"Apparently Seth made himself a private little office," Rob observed.

Excitement revved through Heather's blood as she fingered the black book. This had to be Seth's journal. He'd made himself a small refuge where he could make notes on all he had learned about the illegal drug operation. Heather picked up the book and thumbed through the pages, seeing names and dates and other notations. She wasn't sure what they meant, but she knew she'd found Seth's elusive notebook.

Closing the book and hugging it to her body, she quickly locked the closet back up; then she and Rob went outside. Heather wanted to show Tyler the book right away, but he was still talking on his cell. His gaze met her across the expanse separating them. She patted the book. He gave a thumbs-up sign, then held up a finger, which she figured meant he needed a few more minutes on his call.

Rob's eyes narrowed, making the puckered scars on his face appear molten. "What did you find?"

"Another of Seth's journals." Though it was technically true, she couldn't divulge the uniqueness of this particular notebook. "Did you know he kept journals since he was very young?"

"No, I didn't know."

"Liv found one from his high school years in his things at her town house," Heather said. "Did you know that Seth was driving the car when my parents died?"

Something flashed in Rob eyes. Fear? Dismay? Guilt?

Heather couldn't be sure. Rob seemed to be struggling with some inner conflict.

"Rob?"

Finally he looked up. His twisted and scarred face was awash with regret. "Seth confided in me not long after he was released from the hospital."

Seth had suffered minor injuries. She'd never thought to question why he hadn't been more banged up. The grief of losing her parents, after suffering the loss of Ken, had been almost more than she could bear. Those first few months were a fog. She'd cried herself to sleep many nights.

She pinned Rob with a direct look. "Why didn't you tell anyone?"

"It wasn't my secret to tell." Rob shifted on his cane. "Heather?"

At the sound of her name, Heather turned around to find Liv hurrying toward her. Heather wished she'd thought to hide the book beneath her coat. Hugging it protectively, she smiled as Liv came to a halt in front of her. "Hi, Liv. How was your day?"

Liv's focus was riveted to the book. "What's that?"

"Oh, nothing much. Just a book," Heather said, not wanting to get into a discussion that might lead to revealing what was going on at the tree farm.

"Is it another of Seth's journals?" Liv lifted her gaze.

The hard coldness in her eyes confused Heather. She sought for some way to answer the direct question without lying. Seeing no other option, she said, "Yes, but it's not a personal journal. It's a ledger of farm transactions."

"I want to see it," Liv said and grabbed for the book.

Stunned, Heather tightened her hold on the journal. No way was she giving it up after all the time and energy, not to mention pain, she and Tyler had gone through to find it. Besides, what would Liv want with the book? "Liv, please. This isn't for you."

Liv tugged and twisted. "Give it to me."

"Olivia! Stop." Heather didn't know how else to respond to Liv's childish behavior.

"I want that journal!" Liv raked her fingernails across Heather's knuckle.

"Owww," Heather cried, involuntarily loosening her hold on the book. "Liv, what's gotten into you?"

Rob reached for Liv's arm. "Miss Dorsett, you need to let go."

With Rob's help, Heather regained her grip on the book and wrenched it away from Liv. "Olivia, why are you doing this? What does this book mean to you?"

Rob grabbed Liv again when she raised her arm as if to hit Heather. Liv let out a growl of pure rage and pushed Rob, hard enough that he stumbled to the ground on his unsteady leg. Then Liv ran toward the parking lot, her boots kicking up gravel in her wake.

Heather helped Rob to his feet. After assuring herself he was unhurt, she stared after Liv. She'd parked her car just outside the gate. Her sedan shot forward, spitting gravel as she took off at a fast speed down the village's long drive. Then she hooked a right, tires squealing on the pavement, and disappeared from sight.

"That was so weird," Heather said. "I've never seen her act so…"

"Crazy?" Rob supplied.

"Exactly."

The sound of pounding feet drew her attention. Tyler

and Nathanial ran over to Heather and Rob. "What was that about?" Tyler asked, his eyes dark with concern.

Heather shook her head. Her hand stung where Liv had gouged her. "I think Seth's death is catching up to Liv and making her act out of character. She's usually so composed and elegant."

"She was pretty desperate to get her hands on the book Heather found in the closet," Rob stated. "I don't think it was grief driving her."

Heather stared at Rob. What was he saying? Did he know what the journal contained? Did Liv?

Tyler noticed the book pressed to her chest. "Is that…?"

She said in an even tone, "One of Seth's notebooks."

Understanding and excitement built in his gaze. "Okay. Well, let's get you back to the farmhouse so you can read it."

"Heather, wait." Rob assessed Tyler. "You're not her business partner, are you? You're some sort of law enforcement. DEA?"

Heather's breath hitched. How did he know? Her attention flew to Tyler. The tense line of his jaw hardened his features, and the dangerous glint in his eyes made her want to step back.

"What makes you think that?" he asked.

Tyler's voice was quiet, and yet the sharp, jagged tone sent a shiver down Heather's spine. She'd never seen him like this. This was the cop who brought down drug dealers for a living.

"I'm observant." Rob leaned on his cane. "I've noted you snooping around, asking questions. And if I have, so have others."

"Others like who?"

Heather was glad Tyler asked the question because she wanted to know, as well.

Rob glanced around. "Not here. Let's take this discussion to someplace more private." Rob hobbled away toward the back of the buildings, where there was a small outer building used by the employees during their breaks and lunches. Nathanial was on Rob's heels within seconds.

"Heather, you should stay," Tyler said, holding out his hand for the book. "If this is some sort of trap, I don't want you anywhere near."

Hanging on to the book, Heather shook her head. "No way. I'm not letting this book out of my sight until I've looked through it." She lifted her chin. "Besides, you and Nathanial will protect me."

His mouth pressed into a thin line. "Fine."

She had to double her steps to keep up with his long stride as they made their way to the break house, as the employees affectionately called it. Heather followed Tyler inside and shut the door behind her.

Though it was only the four of them inside the building, Rob pinned her with a direct look and spoke in a low voice. "Do you believe your brother overdosed?"

She inhaled sharply at the question. Her gaze sought Tyler's, but his focus was trained on Rob. She licked her lips and shook her head. "No. I don't."

"He didn't," Rob said with certainty. "I can't prove it, but Seth was in trouble."

She nodded, aware that Tyler's hand rested on the butt of his weapon beneath his shirt and jacket. "What do you know?" she asked Rob.

"I know the people behind his death are ruthless," he answered.

"Do you know who *they* are?" Tyler practically barked at Rob.

"A few months before Seth's death he confessed to me that he'd allowed himself to be roped into permitting the farm to be used by a very vicious drug cartel. He was scared and wanted out but didn't know how to get out from under the bad deal he'd made."

Since it seemed Rob wanted to address only her, Heather asked the question Rob had ignored. "Do you know who on the farm is working for the cartel?"

"I have a few suspicions," he admitted. "But nothing concrete. I didn't want to get involved." He turned to Tyler. "That's why I implored Seth to contact the drug enforcement agency."

A muscle in Tyler's jaw twitched.

"Why didn't you contact the police?" Nathanial asked.

Rob shrugged. "I'm not very popular around here. People believe that I murdered my wife and son. I didn't want to draw any more attention to myself."

Pity stirred in Heather, but she couldn't stop a spurt of anger, as well. If Rob had taken a chance and called the authorities, maybe Seth would be alive. And probably in jail.

"I tried to warn you, Heather," Rob said. "When you returned home, I knew you were in danger."

"You're the one who called?"

He nodded. "Yes." His face twisted. "I'm sorry I didn't do more to help Seth."

Finding compassion within her, she said, "He did listen to you. He called the DEA." She put the book she held on the table. "And he kept records."

"So you two are with the DEA," Rob said.

"I'm DEA. Nathanial is with the Canadian Customs Border Patrol."

"And the other one? Blake?"

Tyler raked a hand through his hair. "ICE."

"I thought so. It seemed a little too coincidental that he had family to visit in Canada."

The excuse Blake used as to why he wanted to drive the refrigerated truck across the border. Unfortunately, their hopes of catching the people waiting for the drugs hadn't panned out. Hopefully they'd find what they needed to take the drug cartel down in the notebook. Heather sat at the table with the journal in front of her. Tyler dragged a chair over to sit next to her. Nathanial leaned over Tyler's shoulder while Rob hung back.

"I should leave you to your investigation," Rob said.

Tyler and Nathanial exchanged a look rife with meaning. Heather supposed the men still didn't trust Rob and were afraid he'd either skip out or tell someone they'd found the book.

"For now, we'd like you to stay," Nathanial said in a tone that left little doubt his words were a command and not a request.

Rob nodded but stayed far back as if getting too close to the book might somehow taint him.

Opening the book, Heather stared at Seth's neat script.

"Look at this." Tyler pointed to the notes. "Seth got names, dates and times. This is great."

Heather wished she could share in his enthusiasm. But seeing the evidence that Seth died to keep hidden only filled her with sadness.

"This is bigger than we thought," Nathanial pointed out. "Look at this. He names the suppliers in California who are bringing in the cocaine from Mexico."

"And here." Tyler's voice echoed with excitement.

"He gives the name and location of the Canadian buyer of the farm's drug-stuffed Christmas trees."

"And look at this." Nathanial pointed to another notation. "Now we know what will be coming in with the balsam fir trees. OxyContin. Didn't Don say that buyers from as far away as California would be picking up their trees?"

"Yes, he did," Tyler said. "We need to bring Don in for questioning." Tyler took a small notebook out of his back pocket and ripped out a page, then twisted in his seat to look at Rob. "I want you to make a list of anyone you suspect might be a part of the drug-smuggling ring."

"Sure, I can do that," Rob said and moved to the other side of the table. He took a pen out of his shirt's breast pocket.

Heather turned the page and froze. The words written there jumped at her. Seth had named Olivia Dorsett, his fiancée, as the US contact for the Mexican drug cartel. Heather's jaw dropped open. *No way. This can't be true.*

Tyler's hand covered hers. "That's unexpected."

But was it? Liv and Seth had met in rehab. She'd ingratiated herself into their family. She probably had seen a perfect opportunity to manipulate Seth into using the farm as cover for the drug cartel. Had she even loved Seth?

Heather's nausea came back full force. She jammed her hands into her pockets to keep from showing how shaky they were. Her fingers flexed, then fisted. A terrifying thought screamed through her brain. Had Liv somehow orchestrated Seth's overdose? Her breath stalled. Spots danced at the edges of her mind.

"I'll let the bosses know," Nathanial said and walked out with his cell in his hand.

Tyler closed the book and put his hand on her shoulder. "Breathe."

Forcing air into her lungs, Heather tried to grapple with the revelations, but her mind didn't want to believe it. "I want to go back up to the house."

"Of course." Tyler helped her to her feet. "We'll stop by the bakery and pick up Colin. He was having a blast when I checked in on him. They were making marzipan."

Before they left the break house, Tyler took the page filled with names from Rob. "Thank you for this. And for trying to protect Heather."

Rob's mouth twisted. "The Larsons are as close to family as I'll ever have."

His words filled Heather with tenderness. She laid a hand over his. "Thank you."

"I'd do anything for you and Colin," Rob said in a voice thick with emotion. "Your parents believed in me when no one else would. I owe them so much."

She nodded. Anxious to get Colin and go back to the house, she left the break house at a brisk walk. The gates were closed and only a few stragglers remained. She entered the bakery with Tyler close behind her.

The bakery was empty.

A tight fist of anxiety slammed into Heather's gut. "Where? Oh, no. Where's my son?"

A banging came from the back of the building. Tyler ran forward. The storage closet where Mrs. Theid kept her supplies was closed, the door locked. From inside, they could hear Mrs. Theid and Deputy Potter.

Tyler broke the lock and opened the door. "What happened?"

Mrs. Theid bustled over to Heather. "It was awful. Seth's fiancée and a nasty man came in with a gun and forced us into the closet."

"Colin?" Tyler asked the question that was lodged in Heather's throat.

Deputy Potter's grim expression didn't bode well. "They took him."

Heather's world shifted. Her knees buckled. Tyler caught her.

Her worst nightmare hadn't prepared her for the searing agony slashing through her. "Liv has my son."

THIRTEEN

Tyler held on to Heather and slowly eased into one of the bakery chairs. Deputy Potter was already on Tyler's phone calling in the kidnapping. The distress of learning that Liv had taken off with Colin swept through Tyler.

He hadn't seen that one coming. Liv had snowed them all with her very convincing act of the grieving fiancée. To think she was the one to orchestrate bringing the drugs into the state of Idaho and using the Larson Christmas tree farm as a way to smuggle illegal substances across the Canadian border boggled the mind. Tyler had to give Seth credit for going against the woman he'd loved by being willing to bring down the cartel. But why hadn't Seth told Tyler Liv was involved? Had he hoped by keeping her part in the drug cartel secret that somehow the authorities wouldn't find out she was in league with the ring and would therefore avoid prosecution?

Tyler crouched down next to Heather and smoothed back a lock of dark hair that had covered her face. Her knuckles turned white with the grip she had on Seth's journal. Her face lost all color, and her breathing was rapid. Shock was setting in. He had to bring her out of it. "Heather, honey, look at me."

She took an audible breath. Fury deepened the color of her eyes. "She has my baby," she ground out. "We have to find her. Now."

Not shock. Fury. A mother's fury. His surprise rapidly morphed into admiration at the fire he saw, hot enough to bring back the color to her face. She was a strong, capable woman with a fierce love for her son. She was a fighter. Good for her. "We will." He almost added *I promise* but they'd already had that conversation. So instead he said, "We'll do everything humanly possible to find Colin. You have to trust me and God."

"I'll try." She stood. "Maybe they're at the house."

He doubted it, but the house was as good a place to start as any.

He escorted her out of the bakery.

Nathanial was finishing up a call and loped over. "The boss is coordinating with the local law and putting out a be-on-the-lookout for Liv."

"She took Colin," Tyler informed him.

Nathanial bared his teeth, a clear sign of his anger. "If she hurts a hair on the child's head…"

"Stand in line," Tyler replied. "We'll make the farmhouse our base of operation."

"Let's go." Nathanial stalked toward where he'd parked the truck.

Tyler and Heather were quick on his heels. Heather slid into the backseat. She was a bundle of nerves if the restless way she tapped her foot and drummed her fingers on her knees were any indication. Not that Tyler blamed her at all. Colin was Heather's world. And she'd trusted Liv. They'd all trusted Liv.

Liv had a lot to answer for. Not only the drug smuggling and Seth's death, but why blow up the propane tank? Why send an armed thug to the house? What was her endgame? Tyler wanted answers. But they had to find her first.

Please, Lord, don't let Liv hurt Colin. Help us find him. Tyler silently prayed the litany over and over again as Nathanial drove them to the farmhouse.

Now Tyler understood why the sting operation in Canada went belly-up. Liv had warned her people there.

Had she also killed Seth by overdosing him with cocaine?

Heather had mentioned Seth had a phobia of needles. It was logical to assume that Liv had somehow incapacitated Seth and then injected him with the drug. Cold-blooded murder.

He fisted his hands with anger at himself for not picking up on Liv's duplicity.

Now the contents of the vial Heather had found took on an even more sinister meaning. The test kit he carried in his travel bag had ruled out cocaine or heroine. He would need to send the vial out for further testing to confirm his suspicion that the white powder inside could possibly be toxic. Considering how Heather had been feeling the past few days, he suspected that Liv had been giving Heather small amounts. Not enough to kill her quickly, just enough to wreak havoc with her system. The question was why?

Dusk bathed the world in shadows and gloom. The snow that had glistened in the light of day had turned icy with the evening temperature dropping. As soon as Nathanial brought the truck to a halt, Heather jumped out. She ran inside, calling Colin's name.

She'd left the journal on the seat. Tyler grabbed it and handed it off to Nathanial. "Can you make a copy?"

"Yep."

Tyler followed Heather inside, dreading the disappointment he knew would come when she realized Liv and Colin weren't there.

He found her in Colin's bedroom. She stood in the middle of the room holding his plush dinosaur. His bed was messy, toys littered the floor and his baby shampoo smell lingered in the air. Tyler's chest tightened.

It tore him up inside to see the distress in her eyes.

"She took some clothes, but she forgot his favorite toy." She took a deep shuddering breath. "Surely she won't hurt him." Tears glittered. "Right?"

Tyler gathered her in his arms. She stiffened and then melted into his embrace, sliding an arm around his waist and laying her cheek against his chest. Tenderness flooded him. He smoothed a hand down her back and wished he had some reassuring words. But he didn't.

Lord, how do I help her?

He breathed in the fresh vanilla scent of her dark hair and closed his eyes. "Please, dear Father in heaven, we pray for protection over Colin. And for help in finding him. We know we can't do this on our own power but by Your might. We ask this in Your precious son's name, amen."

"Amen." Heather lifted her tear-streaked face. "Thank you. I couldn't—" She extracted herself from his arms, lifted her chin and visibly gathered her composure. "How do we track down Liv and bring Colin home?"

That was a question he didn't have a ready answer for. But he made a silent vow to do whatever it took to find her son and reunite him with Heather. He would do anything to make her happy, to take the anguish out of her beautiful eyes.

* * *

Heather paced the dining room as Nathanial and Tyler worked at finding Colin. Both men had phones to their ears and each had a laptop computer open on the dining room table. Tyler had shared that Sheriff Rodriquez had gone to Liv's town house, but she wasn't there. The place had looked as if she'd hurriedly packed up her belongings and fled. The sheriff assured Tyler he'd have an officer watch the place in case Liv showed up.

Though Heather wasn't sure who Tyler and Nathanial were talking to now, she could hear the agitation in Tyler's voice. He was as scared for Colin as she was. And knowing that he cared for her son filled her with affection. But she couldn't shake the sinking sensation that Liv and Colin could be in Canada by now or halfway to Mexico.

This waiting and wondering and not being able to do anything was driving her crazy. Her mind kept playing horrible scenarios like an animation flip book. In each image Colin was scared or hurt and crying for her.

No. No. No. Liv may have betrayed her trust, but Heather couldn't believe that Liv would hurt Colin. But why had she taken him? And where?

To give her hands something to do, she went into the kitchen and made a pot of coffee. She pulled out deli meat and cheeses from the crisper in the refrigerator. Though her hands shook, she set out a snack tray with crackers. Then she began to clean the sink, scrubbing and scrubbing and praying and praying.

Her cell phone rang, making her jump. She quickly grabbed the device from her pocket. The identification bar at the top blocked the caller ID. She answered. "Hello?"

"Don't say a word," Liv's voice spoke into Heather's ear. "If you want to see your son again, don't let your boyfriend the cop know you're talking to me."

Heather's fingers tightened around the phone. She turned away from Tyler. Her first instinct was to do as Liv required of her. But she wasn't good at deception. Hated to be dishonest. Yet her son's life hung in the balance. For Colin she'd walk on hot coals if she had to. Anything for her son.

If she didn't do as Liv demanded, there was a risk she'd never see Colin again. Liv hadn't been bluffing.

Heather's mind told her to go along with Liv, to do as she was told. She had to save her son.

But her heart, her soul, begged her to reconsider. To offer the sacrifice of faith to God. She had to let go of her need to control and trust that God would bring Colin home safely.

Deep inside she knew she couldn't trust Liv.

Tyler had asked her to trust him. He'd said she needed to trust God.

She knew Tyler would comb the earth to find her son.

To do this alone would be foolish. She could end up dead; then Colin wouldn't have anyone to love him.

She met Tyler's questioning gaze across the island counter. She mouthed, *It's Liv.*

He stepped closer and mouthed back, *Speaker.*

Forcing herself to remain calm, she pressed the Speaker button so Tyler and Nathanial could listen. Then into the phone she said, "Hi, Marge, it's been a long time." She hoped Liv bought her pretense of talking to the wife of one of Ken's best friends. "What's up?"

"Listen carefully," Liv said. "In two hours, bring Seth's notebook to this address." She rattled off a street address.

Trembling, Heather fumbled to find a pen and paper in the kitchen utility drawer. Tyler appeared at her side and handed her his pen and notebook. She wrote down the address.

"Come alone," Liv continued. "Or you'll never see your boy again." She hung up.

Heather met Tyler's gaze. "She told me not to tell you. She knows you're law enforcement."

Surprise flared for a moment, then tenderness softened his features. "Thank you for trusting me."

Assured she'd done the right thing, she said, "If I don't show up, I'll never see Colin again."

"That's not going to happen." He pulled her to him and held her tight. "We'll figure this out." He lifted her chin with a finger. "We will get Colin back."

He sounded so sure, so confident. She wanted to believe him. She had to believe him. Believe in him. Otherwise, her life was over. She tugged his face to hers. "I know you will."

Then she kissed him with every ounce of love she could pour into him as if somehow she could give him the power to be the hero she needed.

Deeply touched by Heather's confession, her trust and her kiss, Tyler eased his mouth away and touched his forehead to hers. His breath came in sporadic spurts. Now was not the time to examine why she'd kissed him or what the kiss meant. They had a child to rescue.

With that thought firmly in place, he asked her, "Do you know this address?"

"No." Heather sank onto a chair as if her legs could no longer hold her. "I think it's out by the Boundary County airport off Highway 2."

"Let's call the locals and get some eyes on the place," Tyler said. "They can form a perimeter."

"I mapped it," Nathanial said, pointing to his computer screen. "She's right. It's very close to the airport. Liv must have an exit strategy."

"Call the airport and tell them to ground all planes," Tyler instructed. Seeing how distraught Heather was made him concerned. He needed her to be strong now. "Heather, this is what we're going to do."

She gave him her attention, her hazel eyes wide with fear, but there was enough of the fire left to keep her going. She may have been knocked back a step or two, but she wasn't giving in to despair. He was proud of her. And when the time was right, he'd tell her so.

"You'll drive while Nathanial and I hide in the backseat," he said. "As soon as we're close, we'll jump out and come the rest of the way on foot. You will give Liv the book in exchange for Colin. Once you have him in your grasp, we'll step in and arrest her and her thug."

"That sounds so easy," she said with a faint twist of her lips.

"It won't be. I'm sure Liv will have lookouts anticipating a trap. But we have darkness on our side and night vision goggles so we'll see them even if they see us. It will give us the opportunity to deal with any threats," he assured her. Though the thought of sending her into a dangerous situation by herself made him break out in a cold sweat.

She must have sensed his inner turmoil because she grasped his hand. "You asked me to trust God, remember?"

"Yeah."

"You need to, as well."

He couldn't refute her statement. "You're right." He

lifted her hand and kissed her knuckles. Then he turned to Nathanial. "Can you outfit Heather with coms?"

"You bet," he replied. "Come on over here, Heather. I've got just the thing for a pretty lady like you."

Tyler shook his head at his team member's perpetual charm.

While they were busy wiring Heather with communications so they could hear her and she could hear them, Tyler made plans to make sure Liv and her cohorts wouldn't get away.

He had the feeling there was so much more on the line than he'd ever believed possible.

Heather eased the car to a halt at the entrance of a scrap metal junkyard. She consulted the address Liv had given her just to be sure she was at the right place. She was. "Okay, guys, this is odd."

She'd let the two men out about a half mile back. They were traveling by foot through fields and woods as the crow flew to the drop-off location Liv had specified. The thing Nathanial stuck in her ear crackled; then Tyler's voice filled her head.

"What's up?"

"It's a scrap metal junkyard."

"That's interesting," Nathanial stated. "We'll be there in two minutes."

"What should I do?" she asked.

Tyler spoke, "Go on in. Park near any light that you can find."

"Okay." She stepped on the gas and rolled into the junkyard. She parked beneath a telephone pole that also served as a light source. The place looked deserted. "I don't see anyone."

"Get out and hold up the journal," Tyler instructed.

Taking a fortifying breath, she popped open her door and stepped out of the car, holding Seth's notebook up high.

From the shadows, Liv emerged with a tall muscled man who held a gun to her son's head. Colin's little face was tearstained, his lip quivering. The overhead lamplight reflected off the ring on the man's hand. Heather swallowed her panic.

To hide the fact she was speaking, she put a hand to her mouth as if to cover a gasp of fear she didn't need to fake. "Here she comes," she said. "The thug's got a gun on Colin."

Tyler's voice helped to calm her nerves. "Steady now. Don't give her the book until you have Colin by your side."

Taking a steadying breath and exhaling to keep from giving in to the urge to rip Liv's hair from her scalp, Heather said in a loud voice, "Here's the book. Send Colin to me, and you can have it."

Liv walked forward until she stood a few feet away. "You surprise me, Heather. I figured you'd bring your cop boyfriend." Her eyes glinted with malice. "I guess you aren't as perfect and smart as Seth boasted you were."

"I'm far from perfect, Liv." Heather's gaze lingered on Colin. He was shivering uncontrollably. "Let's get this done. It's cold out here."

Liv held out her manicured hand.

Heather did the same, while keeping the journal tucked at her side. "Give me my son."

Liv harrumphed and gestured for her sidekick to release Colin, who ran full speed for Heather. Needing both hands to gather him close, Heather tossed the notebook at Liv, who fumbled with it. Heather knelt down and hugged Colin to her in a fierce grip. She had her baby back. Nothing else in the world mattered.

"Thank you, Heather," Liv said. "It really is too bad Seth had to go and grow a conscience. I was really looking forward to being a part of your family."

Heather shot her a glare.

Liv shrugged and turned to walk away. "Shoot them both," she said over her shoulder.

Terror streaked through Heather. She pushed Colin behind her and shielded him with her body as the man aimed his weapon at her heart.

FOURTEEN

Hiding behind the stripped-down shell of what used to be a luxury sedan, Tyler's stomach dropped. Liv had just instructed her goon to shoot Heather and Colin. Tyler couldn't let that happen.

The primal instinct to protect the woman and child he loved roared through him.

With a guttural growl, he charged at the thug holding the gun, tackling him before he could pull the trigger. Knocking the goon down to the hard-packed ground, Tyler wrenched the gun from the man and tossed it aside.

This was the same man Tyler had wrestled with before. But this time, nothing could distract Tyler.

His focus had narrowed. Rage infused his body. Adrenaline pumped through his veins as he grappled for dominance over the thug. Landing a hard blow upside the guy's head, Tyler gained the advantage.

Straddling the man, Tyler delivered blow after blow.

No one hurt the people he loved.

Strong arms wrapped around Tyler and lifted him off the now-unmoving thug.

"Stand down, Agent Griffin."

Nathanial's hard voice penetrated through the fog

of fury that had overcome Tyler. He froze, then tapped Nathanial's arm, giving him the signal to release his hold. Nathanial let go and stepped back.

Tyler gathered his control. His chest heaved from the exertion. His heart continued to beat in a sporadic tempo while the adrenaline rush eased, allowing his sanity to return. He held up a hand to Nathanial to let him know he had his self-control back.

"Thanks," he said gruffly to his fellow IBETs member. If Nathanial hadn't pulled him off the thug when he had, Tyler wasn't sure he would have stopped pummeling the guy. "Cuff him."

Nathanial gave a sharp nod, then removed a set of plastic zip ties from his pocket. He flipped the now-moaning goon onto his stomach and tied his wrists and his ankles together.

With his head now clear, Tyler hustled to where Heather, holding Colin, stood. He hated that she'd seen him lose control like that. He never lost control. But he'd never had to defend someone he loved before. This was unfamiliar and scary territory.

"Thank you," Heather said as she threw her free arm around him. "I thought we were going to die."

He gathered them both within his embrace. "I promised you I'd protect you. I always keep my promises."

Heather rose on tiptoe and placed a gentle kiss on his lips. "I know."

His heart squeezed tight. He wanted to bury his hands in her hair and kiss her with all the love he felt, but there was still something he needed to do. "I've got to find Liv."

Heather's eyes rounded. "The journal, too!"

He urged them over to her car. "Get inside, lock the doors and stay down. I'm going after Liv."

Heather placed her hand on his chest. "Don't get yourself killed."

He covered her hand. "I won't. Now inside."

After they were both safely in the car with the doors locked, he withdrew his sidearm and hurried in the direction Liv had disappeared. Once he cleared the light, he pulled the night vision goggles that hung around his neck up so he could proceed into the inky blackness of the junkyard. He moved steadily, searching for any sign of Liv. Toward the back of the junkyard was a mechanic's bay. Light flickered from inside.

Flipping down the night vision goggles, Tyler approached the closed side door. Without hesitation, he kicked the door in, then immediately crouched, making himself a smaller target in case Liv or whoever else was inside took a shot at him.

He rushed into the workshop. In the center was a large metal barrel on fire and Liv was ripping pages from the journal to use as fodder for the flames.

"Liv, it's over," he said as he advanced on her with his weapon aimed at her head. He stayed alert in case another goon was waiting to ambush him.

Seeing him, she tossed the rest of the book in the flames and then gloated, "All your evidence is up in smoke."

"I don't need that book to make sure you end up in jail for a very long time," he countered as he continued to close the distance between them.

"What kind of cop are you?" she asked as she backed away. She jammed her hands into the pockets of her pink coat.

"Show me your hands!"

"Now, now," she said. "No need to be rude." She

withdrew her hands. "You didn't answer my question. Are you FBI, ATF, DEA?"

Not willing to give her the satisfaction of guessing which agency he was with, he said, "It doesn't matter who I work for. What matters is you're going to jail."

Her mouth stretched in a feral grin. "What makes you think you can make any charges stick?"

Behind her, Nathanial entered through another door and slowly moved toward Liv. Wanting to see if he could get more information from her, he gestured for Nathanial to hold up. "Look, tell me who you're working for."

She snorted. "I don't know what you're talking about."

He didn't quibble by arguing with her. She obviously assumed that by destroying the book Heather had given her, they had no information on the drug cartel and no way to connect her to the smuggling ring. He decided to ask something else that was bothering him. "Why were you poisoning Heather?"

"Who says I was?"

"We found the vial of poison," he told her. From behind Liv, Nathanial was ready to apprehend her and gave him a questioning look. Tyler lifted his hand in a subtle gesture to wait. He wanted answers. "You weren't trying to kill her. So I can only guess you wanted her sick enough that she'd have to rely on you."

The way Liv twitched made Tyler believe his guess had hit the mark. "You're the sick one." He tipped his chin, giving Nathanial the go-ahead.

Nathanial holstered his weapon. Then in one fluid motion, he grabbed Liv from behind before she even had time to squawk a protest. The stunned surprise on her face was priceless. While Nathanial quickly secured her wrists behind her back, Tyler recited her Miranda rights.

Together, they escorted her to the main entrance of the junkyard where sheriff's deputies and Bonners Ferry police officers waited for them. The thug was already confined in the back of a cruiser.

As Tyler and Nathanial approached with their suspect in tow, Heather ran from where she'd been talking to the sheriff. Tyler sought out Colin. He was with Deputy Potter.

Heather skidded to a halt in front of Liv. "Liv, why? We trusted you."

Liv's lip curled. "Your mistake. Not mine."

Anger flinted in Heather's eyes, making the green and gold flecks spark. "Where's Seth's journal?"

"Up in flames." Liv's smug tone grated on Tyler's nerves.

Seeing the disappointment marching across Heather's face prompted him to say, "Really, Liv? Did you really think we'd be foolish enough to hand over Seth's journal without making a copy?"

Liv blanched. She bared her teeth at him. "A copy won't hold up in court."

"Maybe not," he said with a shrug. "But that's not something we have to worry about since you burned the copy and we still have the original."

She hissed at him.

"Tell me what happened to my brother," Heather demanded.

"I'm not telling you anything." Liv yanked her gaze back to Tyler. "I want a lawyer."

She was playing this smart. They had her dead to rights with the information in Seth's notebook. "Take her away," Tyler said to the approaching sheriff.

"Please, Liv." Heather blocked their path. "Did Seth really overdose or did you kill him?"

Liv lifted her chin but remained mute.

Heather fisted her hands. "You may think you're clever. But my brother was more so."

Liv sneered. "He was a lapdog, making promises he couldn't keep. He'd have lost the farm if I hadn't bailed him out." She made a disgusted sound. "Get out of my way."

Tyler tugged Heather aside and wrapped an arm around her waist. "Let it go for now," he told her as they watched the sheriff escort Liv to his car, put her in the backseat and shut the door. "We'll eventually get the truth from her. Especially if she makes a deal."

"I guess it's over, then," she said, leaning into him.

"Not quite. There's still the matter of who was working with her on the farm," Tyler said, figuring it was better to let her know what was coming next. She had to be ready to face the fact that another person or persons that she knew and trusted had betrayed her and her brother.

Her weary gaze met his. "Can that wait until morning?"

"I wish it could, but as soon as news gets out that we've arrested Liv, her associates on the farm are going to disappear."

"I understand," she said. "And then what?"

Staring into her beautiful face, he wanted to tell her that he loved her and never wanted to leave her side, but the words stuck in his throat. He couldn't make her any promises. He didn't think he was cut out for a settled domestic life on the farm. He had no skills other than being a cop. And he would never put her and Colin through the agony of disappointment if he couldn't cut it as a father and husband. So instead he said, "With

Seth's journal we'll be able to track down the cartel in the US and on both sides of our borders."

"Do you have to go?" The pleading in her eyes shredded his emotions. "Can't someone else do that?"

He shook his head. "I started this—I need to finish it."

No matter how much he wanted to stay and be the man she needed, he couldn't because he wasn't that man. She needed someone who'd be content working the Christmas tree farm year-round. A man who'd know how to parent a little boy. A man who'd know how to be a good husband to Heather.

Tyler had to seal away his feelings for the widow and son or he might do something foolish and throw caution to the wind and stay.

"What's all this?" From the backseat of her car where she sat with Colin asleep at her side, Heather gaped as they pulled up to the tree farm. The place was ablaze with freestanding lights and a sea of uniformed law enforcement officers was everywhere along with the farm's employees.

Tyler brought the car to a halt at the back of the house. Beside him Nathanial jumped out and hustled around to the front of the house where all the action was going on.

Tyler twisted around to face Heather. "A full-scale investigation is under way. My IBETs taskforce leader is here, along with ATF, ICE, RCMP, DEA and most likely the FBI."

Her head spun with all the acronyms. That was a lot of manpower.

"I told you we would be looking for Liv's cohorts.

Seth's journal gave initials and a few names. But for their operation to have worked, more than a few people were involved. And with the added detail of the fertilizer gone missing, we have to do our due diligence. If a terrorist cell is involved under the disguise of a drug cartel, we need to find out."

The heaviness of distress pressed on her chest. "This keeps going from bad to worse. I'm still struggling to wrap my brain around what Liv did."

Tyler reached over the front seat and took her hand. Their palms fit neatly together. She entwined her fingers through his, wishing she'd never have to let go. But the reality was she'd have to. His job wasn't over. He would follow the trail of the drug cartel, or terrorist cell, or whatever it happened to be. His dedication to serve his country and the people was admirable. Yet she couldn't stop the selfish desire to ask him to give that up and stay with her and Colin. She wouldn't ask, though. For the same reason she'd never asked Ken to give up the military. She never wanted to be the reason they walked away from what they felt called to do. That would only lead to resentment and bitterness down the road. It was better for her, for Colin, to keep her feelings to herself. She smoothed a hand over Colin's dark hair.

"I can only imagine how disappointed and hurt and even angry you are at Liv," Tyler said, drawing her focus back to him. "What she has done is beyond betrayal." He squeezed her hand. "I hope you'll find it in your heart to forgive her."

Taken aback by his words, Heather tried to tug her hand out of his, wanting to break the connection between them. He wouldn't let go. "How can you ask me to forgive her? She used my brother and probably murdered him. She kidnapped my son and would have had us killed if not for you."

"I know it sounds too hard to forgive," Tyler said. "But if you don't forgive her, the anger you feel will turn to bitterness and hate. And that will poison you far worse and faster than the stuff she was giving you."

Heather stared at the night sky. She knew deep in her soul that God would want her to forgive Liv and all of those involved.

But how? Her spirit cried out to God. Aloud she said, "How do I do that?"

Tyler let go of her hand. Startled, she watched him climb out of the car and come around to the back passenger door. He opened it and then crouched next to her and reclaimed her hand. "It's a choice you have to make. Evil is like a cancer. It ravages hearts, minds and souls. Yes, she chose her actions and will pay the price here on earth. But you don't need to pay the price along with her."

He reached up to wipe away a tear. She hadn't even realized she was crying.

She knew the Bible talked of forgiving those who wronged us. Tyler had asked her to trust God. She would have to trust God to help her learn to forgive, as well. She reached to touch Tyler's face. Her emotions swelled to the point where she couldn't contain them any longer. Taking a leap of faith like she'd never taken before, she said, "I love you, Tyler Griffin."

Tyler closed his eyes for the briefest of moments, but she'd seen the stricken expression before his shuttered gaze came back to meet hers.

A knife of pain twisted in her heart, but she wouldn't regret telling him. She dropped her hand. "It's okay if

you don't feel the same. I understand." She gave him a
smile that wobbled despite her attempt to keep it from
doing so. "You've made an impact on my life. And on
Colin's."

"And you both have made an impact on me."

He tipped his chin toward Colin. "Let's get you and
this little guy in the house. I'm sure you must be ex-
hausted, too."

She was, but doubted she'd sleep soundly again for
a long time. She unbuckled Colin's seat belt.

"Here," Tyler said. "Let me carry him in."

Grateful for the offer, she scooted out of the car and
allowed him to scoop Colin up into his arms and carry
him inside to his bed. She followed them.

As Tyler covered Colin with his comforter, she whispered, "Will you stay long enough to say goodbye to
him?"

Tyler put his arm around her waist and led her into
the hall. "I'll be leaving early in the morning. If he's up,
I'll definitely say goodbye to the little man."

"Thank you."

He hesitated as if he wanted to say something. Then a
resigned, stoic expression settled on his handsome face.
"Try to rest. I'll keep everyone out of your hair until
morning. Then you'll be asked questions." He tucked a
lock of her hair back behind her ear, his fingers gently
caressing the line of her jaw before his hand fell back
to his side. "Just tell them what you know. This should
wrap up pretty quickly once everyone has been inter-
viewed."

"How will you get anyone to confess to helping Liv?"

One side of his mouth lifted. "The journal will be a
powerful motivator. My boss has already agreed that

we give everyone an opportunity to come clean for a reduced sentence."

She let out a weary sigh. "I hope they will cooperate."

"It will all work out," Tyler assured her. "By late afternoon tomorrow, your life will resume, and you can move forward."

"But without knowing what really happened to Seth." That burned inside her like a lit match.

"Be patient," he said. "As soon as Liv breaks, and she will—they always do—I'll send word."

Be patient. That would be a test. "I should let you get to it, then."

"Yes. I'll see you in the morning." He left, his footsteps echoing in the quiet house.

Heather made herself crawl into bed. She did need rest. Tomorrow would be grueling. In so many ways. Sleep came quickly, and so did the morning.

The aroma of fresh-brewed coffee wafted upstairs, stirring her awake. She dressed, choosing a pair of stretch jeans in a dark wash, a green sweater that she knew brought out the green in her eyes and short boots. She combed her hair into bouncy waves and put on just the barest hint of mascara and lip gloss. If she had to say goodbye to Tyler, she wanted him to remember her like this and not in her baggy sweats. She checked on Colin. He was still fast asleep. She headed downstairs and found Tyler sitting at the dining table with a cup of coffee.

He rose as she entered. The appreciation in his gaze brought heat to her cheeks. "Hope you don't mind, but I helped myself to some coffee."

Her heart thumped. He looked so handsome in his cargo pants and black T-shirt. His dark hair was damp from a recent shower and his jaw clean-shaven. She could smell the spicy aftershave he used. She imprinted the scent in her mind. "Not at all."

"I hung Seth's coat in the hall closet."

"Thank you."

"Crime scene techs will need to collect Liv's things that she left in Seth's room."

"Okay."

"Is Colin still sleeping?"

Hoping her son wouldn't feel the disappointment of Tyler leaving as keenly as she did, she said, "I'll tell him you said goodbye."

An awkward silence descended between them.

Finally, he held out his hand. She grasped it like a lifeline.

"I have to go now," he said.

Her heart cried out, *No!* She put on a brave smile. "I'll walk you out."

He opened the front door, and they stepped out onto the porch. He drew her close and pointed up to the sprig of mistletoe hanging over their heads.

This time she didn't run away. She wasn't sure if she moved first or if he did, but they met in a fiery kiss that curled her toes and left her breathless.

Uncertainty shone in his eyes. "I'll keep in touch, okay?"

She wasn't sure she could stand the torture of hearing from him without being able to see him. "Would you like to spend Christmas here? We'd love to have you."

A pained expression crossed his features. "As much as I'd like to say yes, I have no idea where I'll be at Christmas. I can't make any promises to you, Heather."

Though he didn't say it, she heard the unspoken *Not now, not ever.*

Needing to be strong for him and herself, she stepped out of his embrace. She had to send him on his way and make sure he didn't see how torn up inside she was. Forcing her voice to an even tone, she said, "Then I wish you well, Agent Tyler Griffin."

"Goodbye, Heather."

He walked away, taking her heart with him.

FIFTEEN

Tyler hunkered down inside the small confines of a battered surveillance van. He was parked in an alley outside of the known hangout of a major drug dealer, a nightclub in central Los Angles.

It had been nearly a month since he'd left Idaho; following the information in Seth Larson's journal had led to a successful closure to the case. The IBETs force had confiscated thousands of dollars' worth of cocaine, made multiple arrests, closed off this particular Mexican pipeline of illegal drugs both in the US and Canada.

The Mexican authorities were cracking down on the members of the drug cartel's operatives that the Border Service had shared with them.

It was Christmas Eve, and as he had for every major holiday, with the exception of the wonderful Thanksgiving he'd spent at the Larson Christmas tree farm with Heather and Colin, Tyler had volunteered for tonight's assignment. Doing so meant another man could spend the time with his family.

Never before had Tyler begrudged his career choice. Never before had he felt restless on a stakeout with questions bombarding him. Had he done the right thing by not telling Heather he reciprocated her love? He'd walked away, allowing her to believe he didn't love her. Which was so not the truth. He loved her. Loved her in a way he had never loved anyone else. Sure, he'd dated and he'd had relationships, but he'd always bailed when things became too emotional. Too complicated.

Just as he had with Heather.

He was an idiot. He didn't want to be here tonight. Or tomorrow on Christmas Day, if the drug deal that the information grid indicated went down.

"We've got a live bogey coming your way," the voice of his fellow DEA agent, Paul Summers, came over the radio. Paul was in another vehicle on the main thoroughfare with a clear view of the alley entrance.

Tyler snapped to alertness. Through the dingy front windshield of the van, he saw a figure scurrying down the alley. "On it."

He grabbed the camera and snapped pictures. He couldn't move in until he saw an exchange of drugs. And if the deal went down inside, he'd have to wait for the players to leave before busting them.

"What's happening?" Paul asked, his voice sounding a bit garbled. Probably from the cheeseburger dinner Paul always had on stakeouts. The man lived on fast food.

"Not much," Tyler replied. Weary, he set the camera aside to take a swig of water.

"Well, I wish they'd get on with it," Paul groused. "My old joints are getting stiff sitting here."

Like him, Paul was single and worked the holidays. Paul was fifteen years Tyler's senior.

It occurred to Tyler in a brief moment of clarity that with the way things were going, he would be Paul in fifteen years. Alone and sitting in a too-small car on Christmas Eve waiting for some criminal element to make his day.

"I'm done," he said aloud. He didn't want this life anymore. He wanted to be with Heather and Colin. Though he knew they were doing all right without him. He'd kept tabs via Deputy Potter, who had agreed to regularly check in at the farm. But Tyler needed Heather and Colin in his life. He loved them both and wanted nothing more than to spend Christmas with them.

"What's that?" Paul asked.

Tyler watched the suspect enter the building, the door closing firmly behind him. "Tonight's stakeout is a dud. Guy disappeared inside. I'm calling it."

Meaning he was packing up shop and would hand the case over to someone else. For Tyler tonight was the beginning of what he hoped would be a wonderful life.

"Mommy!" Colin jumped onto Heather's bed, waking her from a sound sleep. She sat up to smile at him. He was dressed in his rocket pj's, his dinosaur hung from his hand and his little face was lit up like a Fourth of July sparkler. "It's Christmas morning! Happy Birthday, Jesus!"

"Yes, it sure is." Instead of pretending that Santa was real and leaving presents under the tree, she'd taught Colin that the giving of gifts to each other was an expression of love following God's example of giving humanity Jesus. "Shall we sing happy birthday to Jesus?"

"Not without the cake!"

They'd baked a carrot cake with cream cheese frosting, Colin's favorite. They would put candles on it and blow them out together.

"Okay, sweetie, give Mommy just a minute to wake up."

"Can I go look at the presents?"

She smiled as love crowded her chest. "Yes. After you brush your teeth."

"I already did." He crawled over to her and breathed his minty breath in her face. "Smell."

She laughed and hugged him tight. "Okay, smart boy. You can go downstairs. Just don't open any presents until I get there."

"I won't." Colin bounced off the bed and ran out of the room. His feet pounding down the stairs reverberated through the house.

Heather flopped back for a moment. She hadn't been sleeping well this past month. Nightmares of Liv and her thug disturbed her rest. Many times in the middle of the night Heather would reach out, calling Tyler's name, and she'd awaken knowing he wasn't there. She hadn't heard from him since a week after arresting Liv.

He'd called to tell her that Liv had cracked, like he'd predicted. She'd admitted to injecting Seth with a lethal amount of cocaine. She'd also stated she'd wanted Heather sick so that she could ingratiate herself more firmly on the farm.

It had been so good yet so distressing to hear Tyler's voice. She'd wanted to beg him to come back. She hadn't. He had a life that didn't include her and her son. End of story.

But today she wouldn't think about the heartache that throbbed within her chest. Today she'd concentrate on her son. She threw back the covers and changed from her pajamas into her comfy sweats. She swept her hair up into a loose ponytail and brushed her teeth.

The tune of "Jingle Bells" filled the house.

She groaned. Who would be coming to visit on Christmas morning? She wasn't expecting anyone. She padded downstairs in time to see Colin streaking across the hardwood floor toward the front door.

"Colin, no." She hurried down the last few stairs and rounded the corner just as Colin yanked open the door.

Tyler stood on the other side of the threshold, looking so handsome in pressed khaki slacks, a button-down shirt beneath a down jacket. He held a bag of presents in one hand and a bouquet of red and white roses in the other. His gaze collided with her, knocking the breath from her lungs and sending her senses reeling. He was here. Really here. She pinched herself to make sure she wasn't dreaming.

"Mr. Tyler!" Colin cried and flung himself at Tyler's legs, hugging him tightly.

Stunned, Heather moved to him. She blinked back the tears burning her eyes.

"What are you doing here?"

He gave her a lopsided grin. "There's nowhere on earth I'd rather be on Christmas than here with you two." He held out the flowers.

She took them and buried her nose in the fragrant blooms to hide her confusion and delight.

"Hey, squirt." Tyler easily lifted Colin with one arm. "I missed you."

Colin flung his arms around Tyler's neck. "We missed you."

Heather met Tyler's gaze. He arched an eyebrow. "Is that so?"

"Yes. We missed you."

His smile could have lit up all the United States. "Good."

Setting Colin down, Tyler entered the house and shut the door.

"Are those for us?" Colin asked, pointing to the bag of presents.

"They are." He handed Colin the bag. "Can you put them under the tree?"

Colin grabbed the bag and dragged it into the living room where their large Douglas fir, decorated with a ton of ornaments and multicolored lights, stood in front of the living room window.

Tyler closed the distance between him and Heather. Though he didn't touch her, his gaze was a soft caress that sent a delicious shiver down her spine.

"I love you, Heather Larson-Randall. And I want to spend the rest of my life with you, if you'll have me."

"What about your career?" Surely he wasn't leaving law enforcement for her. She couldn't allow that because one day he might come to resent her for it.

"Seems the sheriff's department is in need of someone with my experience and background."

Overcome with joy, she circled her free arm around his neck and pulled him closer. "Yes. Oh, yes, I'll have you. I love you." She pressed her lips to his in a soul-searing kiss.

"Hey, you're not under the mistletoe," Colin chided.

They broke the kiss with laughter filling their hearts.

Colin bounced on his feet. "Can we open presents now?"

Filled with love and gratitude, Heather thanked God for giving her the best gift ever—a wonderful son and a man to love for eternity.

* * * * *

Dear Reader,

I hope you've enjoyed the third book in the Northern Border Patrol series. I love writing Christmas stories because the time of year when we celebrate the birth of Jesus is so very special to me. Setting this book on a Christmas tree farm gave me a way to bring in DEA agent Tyler Griffin on the trail of a drug-smuggling ring. Pairing him with widow Heather Larson-Randall was a perfect fit.

Heather needed to open her heart up to a second chance at love, but trusting both Tyler and God didn't come easy for her. When she finally was ready to put her trust in Tyler and God, she was able to have her happy ending, despite the danger that threatened her and her son's life. Tyler arrived at the farm never expecting to fall in love with Heather. He wrongly believed he wasn't husband or father material. But throughout the story his actions proved how wrong his belief was. And when he finally opened up to the love Heather offered, he realized that he was the perfect man for Heather and her son.

I hope this holiday season finds you with the ones you love and that the true meaning of Christmas will open your hearts to God's love.

Look for the next two Northern Border Patrol books coming in 2016.

Also keep an eye out for the new continuity series from Love Inspired Suspense—Rookie K-9 Unit: brave rookies and their loyal dogs serve and protect. This continuity will run from April 2016 to September 2016. I'll be writing book 1!

Until next time, may God bless you and keep you in His care.